Stories No One Hopes
Are about Them

Iowa Short Fiction Award

Stories No One Hopes Are about Them

by A. J. Bermudez

University of Iowa Press · Iowa City

University of Iowa Press, Iowa City 52242
Copyright © 2022 by A. J. Bermudez
uipress.uiowa.edu
Printed in the United States of America

Text design and typesetting by Sara T. Sauers
Printed on acid-free paper

This is a work of fiction. Any similarity to actual persons or
events is purely coincidental.

Library of Congress Cataloging-in-Publication Data
Names: Bermudez, A. J., 1987– author.
Title: Stories No One Hopes Are about Them /
by A. J. Bermudez.
Description: Iowa City: University of Iowa Press, [2022]
    Series: Iowa Short Fiction Award
Identifiers: LCCN 2022015161 (print) |
    LCCN 2022015162 (ebook) |
    ISBN 9781609388638 (paperback; acid-free paper) |
    ISBN 9781609388645 (ebook)
Subjects: LCGFT: Short stories.
Classification: LCC PS3602.E7589 S76 2022 (print) |
    LCC PS3602.E7589 (ebook) | DDC 813/.6—dc23/eng/20220408
LC record available at https://lccn.loc.gov/2022015161
LC ebook record available at https://lccn.loc.gov/2022015162

for Ruth

Contents

The Real India . . . 1

Obscure Trivia of the Antarctic . . . 25

Octopus . . . 42

Casualty . . . 55

Bottle Girl . . . 59

Ori Dreams of a Tree . . . 71

All the Places You Will Never Be Again . . . 74

Insertion . . . 78

Cain vs. Cain . . . 80

The Body Electric . . . 83

The Lady Will Pay for Everything . . . 90
ދަވަނަޖޮ ޒުރިޔާ އާރުކޮނަރ ވާސިރ ދިހަހާނު

Eating the Leaves . . . 98

Mnemophobe . . . 100

Orphan Type . . . 103

Lacquer . . . 113

The Train Speaks . . . 115

Picking the Wound . . . 118

Totenhaus . . . 120

Retrospect . . . 127

Year of the Snake . . . 131

Stories No One Hopes
Are about Them

The Real India

THE CENTERPIECE OF Lark's studio is the *Cunt Bodhisattva*, an eight-foot architectural marvel of sedimentary vermiculite clay, sustainably retrieved from someplace in South Africa, molded in the shape of a woman bent over backward in an Ūrdhvadhanurāsana pose, feet planted, vagina spread and on display, stomach arching toward buoyantly upside-down tits and a neutral, choiceless face, palms firm on the ground astride a thicket of load-bearing hair.

"What do you think?" Lark asks.

"I think it's a striking confluence of the obverse elements of female fetishization and empowerment."

"I want her to feel *playful*. Does she feel playful?"

"She does."

"Really?"

"Extremely playful."

"Mark hates it."

"Of course Mark hates it," I say. "Mark's the embodiment of the white male heteronormative art complex." Lark nods. These are words she knows. "He lives in fear that the Paleolithic Venus sculptures he curates will come to life in the night and strike a pose like this one."

"She doesn't look frightening?"

"Frightening how?"

"Like is her pussy the right shape?"

I look, really look, at the docile squiggles of the labia, the pinch of the clitoral hood, and the pearl of clay beneath, the elegant, apologetic dot of the urethra, all probably carved by her assistant Andrew, who's here on a fragile O-1B visa, and say, "There is no right shape." Lark nods, pleased but not sold. "But yes, it's a beautiful pussy."

She smiles. "I think so too."

When she begins to understand something like this, something she's made, you can't help but believe that it's your fault. You've taught her the words for this, penned index cards thick with the micro-vocabularies of feminism and post-feminism and post-post-feminism. You've gently guided the pronunciation of *eurocentrism, hegemony, intersectional transmedia narrative*. You've tenderly explained why *transgender* is apropos and *tranny* is verboten. Have explained why *hermaphrodite* is fine for bivalve mollusks and Herculine Barbin circa 1856 but not for humans who contemporarily identify as intersex.

"Why?" she's said. "Why though *really*?"

"Because a community decides what they want to be called."

She accepts this and will regurgitate it back to a curator sometime. You've prepped her for this, marked the signposts of Native to Indigenous to First Peoples, POC to BIPOC to People of the Global Majority. You've explained what each letter of LGBTQIA+ and QUILTBAG signifies. She's exhausted by the quantity but eager to learn, consults the cheat sheet you've made for her. You've walked around the studio, sidestepping the massive swaths of canvas drying on the floor, admiring whatever's been pinned to the wall as a kind of low-key test, and discussed her work in terms she'll adopt and re-present: the homages to Nan Goldin and Laura Mulvey, the dovetailings with Nam June Paik and Mika Rottenberg. The sentences, read and reread, meticulously memorized until someone else's words sound like they've lived in her mouth for years, the soundbites that will make it seem like she's read the whole thing.

It occurs to me, often, that I'm a traitor to the authors of books she hasn't read, the artists who couldn't afford the buy-in, the other artists whose work has nothing to do with her work but whose catalogs are referenced in her list of influences; to women, to PhD candidates, to people whose last name ends in –*ez,* like mine.

Nonetheless, I cash the checks, and this is the thing that Lark has always understood. To be paid for something is to consent to it. To endorse it, as it were.

One day, between the vat of drying resin and the overexposed photographs, Lark says: "Let's go to India."

On its surface, this exclamation has the pastiche of a whim, but if you listen closely, you can hear the machinations. The impulse is spontaneous in the way that midcentury housewives would sometimes, suddenly, fully out of the blue, swallow dishwashing liquid instead of rosé.

"I have the miles," she says. "Enough for two seats in first."

Already I can imagine the thrill and stress of it. Unfettered access to the finer things, with Lark watching every selection like she's keeping score. How chic you are, how worldly you are, how alcoholic you are. How many times you've done this before (if none, a rube; if several, then why are you working for her?). She enjoys introducing people to things, like how the vegan meal is unfailingly better than the chicken or steak option, even if you eat meat, because it's rarer and more intentionally prepared. But sometimes she grows weary of her calling as a missionary of prestige and simply gifts you a copy of *Tiffany's Table Manners for*

Teenagers, because, as we all know, you'll never be taken seriously if you hold your fork wrong.

She likes you to wear good clothes, but she likes to come up with them. She brings you the latest issue of *Vogue*, asks you to circle what you're attracted to. You select safely. You are good at tests, but there's no timer set, no rubric. No rules. When she finally returns, she looks at your selections. After each, she nods or tilts her head. "No," she says, more jaded than critical, "not for your shape."

She listens raptly to your stories of travel, stories she's asked to hear, threshing them for points of interest, exotic kernels of potential that prove how interesting you are. Occasionally she lights up and ends stories for you with a single, often incorrect sentence like "So you hopped the next flight and came home immediately" or "But *that's* the brother you lost your virginity to."

She takes you to a cake restaurant, exactly what it sounds like, right after she's hired you, and buys you a slice of cake. Ten feet from your table, a baby shower is in the throes of learning how to make custom cakes from a comically good-looking instructor, all elbow-deep in nonpareils and piping paraphernalia and strips of festively tinted fondant. Lark, who's been laughing and waving her thin arms around and talking about the importance of eating cake, how you only live once, sets down her fork and takes your chin in her hand. "Oh," she says. You've also stopped eating cake, since your chin is no longer your own. "You know, you can get almost anything done in LA," she says. "Anything. Places are so good here. It's amazing." Then, because you might not have understood, "Laser hair removal treatment," she says.

You don't brief her on your awareness of the field, your extensive history of borderline-unaffordable Groupons or the realities of genetics extending through your maternal and grandmaternal lineage presumably back to the Iron Age, when this flaw presumably indicated some now-defunct evolutionary advantage. You don't tell her you're doing your best, and you don't cry in the cake restaurant. "Thank you," you say instead.

Every time you're dressed wrong, for years, you blame the East Coast. "It's a different aesthetic," you say, as though you're still getting the hang of things here in cryptic LA. As though you could afford the low-rung sample sale shift dresses and harem pants, all size zero or zero-adjacent, one-size-fits-all, "all" being a subgroup to which you apparently don't belong.

She tells you, on one occasion, about her abortion, and all you can think is *That's probably for the best.*

Lark is insistent on the *real* India, not the postcard India or the *Darjeeling Limited* India, the tourist India or Hilton India. She's been before, multiple times, years ago. She says her soul is there. She hopes to be buried there.

You know that you will never go to India without Lark.

So you say yes.

The night before our departure, I stay up till sunrise, an attempt to acclimate myself to the new time zone—the exact opposite of Los Angeles—and to sleep through the flight. When I wake up in first class, Lark's fallen asleep beside me, and I take the opportunity to order a scotch. "Poison," she'd say, were she awake, although the first thing she'll do when we land is find and buy heroin. By the time she wakes up, I've had two glasses of scotch and swapped the glass out for a cup of tea. She immediately, briskly summons a flight attendant, as though she's been waiting all this time, and orders two flutes of champagne. "Live a little," she says, handing my mug of tea to the attendant with the lithe, performative grace of a fairy godmother.

When the champagne arrives, Lark studies it and then smirks, like she'll allow it. "Not real," she says. "What's that word?"

"Ersatz," I say.

"That's right. *Ersatz* champagne." It's clear now, with twelve collective ounces of brut or blanc de blancs or whatever bubbling before us that Lark has set me up. That whatever she says next will have the de facto portent of a toast. "I've been thinking," she says, "about the *real* reason for India." She leans in, conspiratorially. "It's the *Cunt Bodhisattva*. Imagine her sixty feet tall, arched over the border between Jammu and Kashmir, half her body in one state and half in the other, her belly button skyward right at the border. Body the same color as the sand."

I nod and, because I'm exhausted and secretly drunk and trapped on this airplane, I say, "Yes. Of course yes. You're a genius."

"You get it though, right?"

"Of course. It's the interstice of postcolonial conflict literally embodied by the intrinsically female dichotomy of religious idolatry: the contraposed irony of deification and objectification."

Lark smiles, lifts her glass. "Exactly."

Of course it's work. It was always going to be work.

Lark's hired a driver, and the moment we get in the car, you can tell it's only a matter of time before she fucks this guy. He introduces himself as Sai, a name she leans forward and asks him to sound out twice, despite its being only one syllable. Sai gratifies her request, foreplay-slow, then smiles like the bushes are full of paparazzi. The way he smiles, the snug fit of his Henley, you can tell Sai understands how money works.

Lark settles into the seat beside me and says, "Remember what I said back in LA?"

I do. I remember everything, although I'm not sure to what she's referring.

"White linen," she says, and when she looks at you she closes her eyes, maybe imagining something else. Some other you. "You have white linen, right?"

"I do."

Lark leans back, briefly closing her eyes again, maybe this time in a small expression of gratitude to the universe, and says, "This is going to be an electric trip."

Her hand is still on my knee, fingers polished with a color that is the exact same shade as her actual nails, and she's right, I guess, I am wearing black, all black, which is not what we've discussed, and although laboriously selected and tested for chicness and comfort and some je ne sais quoi factor that's really only ever a guess, at best, it is 100 percent the opposite of what we'd talked about, and in a way, she's extra right because I'm noticing it for the first time now too.

On the half-hour drive from the airport to Haveli Dharampura, Lark leans against the window, enraptured by some frequency I can't hear. In the narrower side streets—shortcuts, Sai avers with a wink—people turn and look through the untinted back windows of the car. Lark is making eye contact with as many people as she can. Her soul is here, so I guess she knows what she's doing. I feel a pang of the same schadenfreude I get sometimes in Venice, seeing the tourists lifting cameras on straps around their necks, dodging skateboards, huddling over one iPhone to compare restaurant reviews, although now I'm the tourist and there's no joy, so it's really just shaden sans freude.

"What do you think?" says Lark. Her eyes are shining, and in this moment I wonder if I've just missed her all this time. If perhaps she was right all along, a savant for the things that are ugly and aren't, correct and incorrect, repugnant and resplendent. Maybe I read too much. Maybe I don't read the right things. Maybe, in this place, in the unpredictably scrawled circle of her magic, I can contort and flourish into some other thing.

"I'm so happy I'm here," I say. And I am. "Thank you."

I squeeze her hand and she squeezes back. She smiles, and I feel myself breathe into a part of my chest I haven't felt in weeks. I'm exhausted, dehydrated, and nauseous from the ride, but she—this—is how the sun is. When it shines, it shines hot.

Through the meticulously clean glass of the backseat windows, I try to see the world as Lark does. Low-slung blocks of concrete scroll past, ribboned with patches of color and signage, carts and bikes, smoke and sound, and I wonder if these are, to her, the real India. The window is cold against my forehead, and my eyes keep slipping closed. Despite what looks like a cacophony of sensory detail, all I can smell is the pine of the air freshener, fake as grape candy, and the delicate bite of Sai's aftershave.

We're six minutes into the ride when Lark leans forward, touches Sai where his deltoid meets his biceps, and asks, in a way I recognize from the DeVotchKa concert in Las Vegas, the balcony of The Box in New York, the parking lot outside the Nordic Pavilion at the Berlin Biennale, in a manner at once sexy and inarticulate, where she can score some black tar heroin.

The hotel is a masterpiece, blessed by UNESCO, and though it's been in play for two centuries, Lark still looks over her shoulder as we ascend the steps, immensely self-satisfied, as though she discovered it. "See?" she says. I nod, doing my best to look enchanted.

Behind us, illegally parked along the too-narrow street nearest the entrance, Sai unloads our luggage. As I turn he winks, and it's unclear whether this gesture represents a stray bit of buckshot from his tactical flirtation or a private, conspiratorial acknowledgment of our member-hood in the same servant class.

A concierge and team of receptionists, all clad in white linen with brightly colored nylon vests, are poised to greet us in the lobby. I wonder if the different vest colors denote different teams or roles, like in kickball or an Atwood novel. Lark places her palms together and lightly bows to everyone at once. I abstain, feeling in this gesture the same discomfort I've felt at the end of yoga classes in West Hollywood amid an ocean of balayage, all blond and blond-adjacent, pre- and post-blond, women netting six figures per annum from their first divorces and more recent real estate licensures, reverently whispering *namaste* to one another. This, I'm quite certain, is not the real India. In any case, we've arrived.

As we receive our keys, Sai confers with a bellhop, ensuring that our luggage will arrive at the rooms before we do. Lark has been rattling off the names of local specialties, none of which I'll remember. "Let's have dinner on the roof," she's saying. "Seven or eight. Eight is better." I nod, with the tacit understanding that I'll hang back and make the reservation. "Don't sleep," she advises. "You'll want to." I nod at this too—she's not wrong, this is the core principle of outwitting jet lag—although the only thing I've been able to think of since the flight is a nap.

After making arrangements for dinner with the concierge, I head up to my room and lie down. The bed is a mint-green queen, nested beneath a scalloped interior archway, one among a sprawling conundra of scalloped interior archways, facing a simple flatscreen TV. On the balcony, two small rattan chairs overlook a spacious multistory court-yard—the jewel of the hotel's internet presence—and flank a small outdoor table, exactly the right size for a pot of tea with two cups and saucers. The bathroom, which I've only visited to splash cold water on my face, is white faux marble with touches of brass, complimentary toiletries and washcloths all the same shade of faded persimmon.

I lie on top of the duvet to avoid any imprints on my skin from the seams of the sheets, pull my hair upward from the nape of the neck to ward off the telltale flatness of the hair, indisputable evidence of napping. I close my eyes, but have set a timer for fifteen minutes. Lark used to model, ages ago, to what degree I'm unsure (there's been mention of a Pepsi ad), but to a sufficient extent that she knows, as surely as an MD with a stethoscope clocking a heartbeat, when anyone has taken a nap. "It's in the eyes," I've heard her say, "You can tell," although I myself cannot. I don't know if it's a puffiness akin to the aftereffects of drinking or a hot shower, if either of these would enhance or negate the appearance of a nap, so I do nothing. My top priority is to stay awake, against all odds, so that I can appear to be awake.

When the alarm goes off, I pull a set of white linen clothing—drawstring pants and a tunic top—from my suitcase, hang the ensemble on the rod of the shower, and turn on the water as hot as it will go to steam out the creases. This is among the few pieces of sartorial intelligence I've arrived with on my own, uninherited from Lark.

Hers is the room next to mine, and when there's a knock on her door I jolt. I relax upon hearing the door open, then the sound of chatter,

Lark's laugh. In nondescript language sounds: an invitation. In nondescript language sounds: a polite decline. The door, again.

Dinnertime is the equivalent of dawn in Los Angeles. Lark arrives fifteen minutes past seven o'clock, relaxed and wise in a way that suggests she's smoked a half gram of heroin. Everywhere there are tiny scallops in the walls, each set with a tea light. Each glints off her eyes the way that fire licks and then swells against the window of a burning building.

"You were gone a long time," she says.

I've only been in my room, timing everything out, but "Yes," I say, "it's been a long time."

I order the things from the menu that I think I remember her saying, but nothing is right. She presses the plump exterior of every object that arrives, pale beige nail against pale beige skin against pale beige dough, with the pad of her index finger, testing each piece, then ripping a section of food from its body and setting it aside, like she's done it a favor.

"You don't seem happy," she says. But I am happy. I'm plenty happy— not heroin happy, of course—but happy.

"I'm just quiet," I say. "Happy quiet."

Lark nods, dissecting another roll with her fingers. "Tomorrow we'll find a musician," she says. "We should have done it already."

This impulse, something she apparently picked up on a previous excursion, is one I've been dreading. In the days leading up to the trip, she's often hailed the importance of hiring a driver, then a musician, as the only real way to travel through India. "Should we ask Sai if he knows someone?"

Lark looks at me like I'm insane. "No," she says, "it's essential to get a vibe."

The sun has only just set, but the sky to the west has turned a violent orange, leaking upward toward a murky swath of liatris blue, looking less like an actual sunset and more like a cocktail named after one. "I photographed the light here once," she says. "Before your time. Leica, obviously. I blew the image up to four thousand percent. *Four thousand.* Huge." She bobs a dead bag of English breakfast tea in the silty, tepid water of her china cup. "Artists do that now—you saw that fucking shit at Barry-Platte last fall—*I* came up with that."

"I've seen the photographs. They're beautiful."

Lark's expression stiffens, like I'm not getting it. Like no one is. She suddenly looks extraordinarily tired, a bit confused, like a baby that's about to cry. "Nature belongs to all of us," she says, eyes glassily fixed on a sherbet-hued minaret. "People think nature belongs to no one, but that's not true. It belongs to all of us."

She sits back from the table. On her plate, the mauled corpse of a dosa, translucent and jettisoned like the skin of a snake, sits hollowly amid a bay of decorative cilantro.

"In the morning," she says, apropos nothing, part promise, part threat.

She tosses her cloth napkin onto the plate and three servers appear as if by magic, clearing the table with the alacrity of mafia novitiates purging a crime scene.

In the morning, the sky has turned from bruise-black purple to a scabbed-over white-gray. Lark has a headache, so we meet on her balcony for breakfast, avoiding the clattering dishes and silverware of the restaurant. "So," she says, "what are we going to do about this statue?"

"Well, first thing is to find a fabricator."

Lark nods. She pensively rips apart a ball of idli, sets the pieces back down on her plate. "And we'll need a clay guy."

"Do you know anyone? Here?"

Lark smushes a wad of idli between her fingers, then brightens with what must be a wonderful idea. "Let's ask Sai!" she says. "I'll bet Sai knows someone."

"Okay," I say.

Sai, to my chagrin, does know someone. His "clay guy," one of many stars in the constellation of Sai's rolodex, will laugh, bewildered and overjoyed by the project—he, too, "would enjoy seeing a pussy of this magnitude"—before recommending that the body of the *Cunt Bodhisattva* be constructed in eight parts: two arms, two legs, the upper torso, the middle torso, the lower torso/nethers, and the head. He will painstakingly coat the conglomerations of metal and wire crafted by the fabricator, an underpaid sophomore at the Delhi School of Art, before loading and transporting all eight sections of the eponymous Bodhisattva via convoy through the tortuous curves of Himachal Pradesh to the border of Kashmir and Jammu, some middle-of-nowhere set of coordinates I've been tasked with identifying through a combination of Google map searches and hearsay, where we are unlikely to be disturbed by armed guards (fingers crossed), before assembling, photographing, and generally reveling in the majesty of the statue and all it exemplifies before returning to our boutique hotel in Udhampur.

But first, before any of this, we must find a musician.

As we near Connaught Place, Lark lowers the backseat window of the car and props her elbows against the window frame. She leans out, eyes closed, and inhales deeply. Amid the cacophonics of the milieu—bicycles, carts, vendors, children—she perks up at some sound: an egregiously out-of-tune sitar, stabbing at a melody that sounds a bit like "Over the Rainbow."

She asks Sai to pull over and, sussing out the source of the sound, approaches an older gentleman who has what she'll describe as a "kind face." From the car, I watch with Sai as Lark speaks to the man slowly and clearly, bent at the waist in the posture of a black-and-white film heroine, couture-clad on a visit to the orphanage, dripping with beatific elegance and the salvific promise of white picket fences, hydrangeas, suburban reincarnation. The man is dressed in white linen and loose sandals, a weathered sitar nested in his lap. He nods as Lark draws a map in the air with the full length of her arms, then smiles, creases bundling along his eyes and mouth. He does, indeed, have a kind face. At last, the man gets to his feet and follows Lark to the car.

As we pull onto Ghanta Ghar Road heading east, Lark turns backward in her seat and places a hand on the musician's knee. "Play something, Rishi," she says.

Rishi dutifully plays a warbling riff, the neck of the sitar bobbing toward the roof of the car. Lark seems rapturously oblivious to the sourness of the instrument's tuning. Or perhaps this is why she chose him. Perhaps this is the real India.

Sai and Lark are in their own world up front, the principal cast of a madcap road trip. Lark leans against the glass with her chin tilted at an attractive angle, a pose of extremis, lips ever-so-slightly parted. You can almost imagine the Pepsi dripping directly into her mouth. Sai glances her direction from time to time, aware of the bait, taking the bait.

Lark and I went sailing once, with her then-husband and my then-girlfriend, and this is the face I remember, tilted expectantly toward the sun, Ferruzzi's *Madonnina* by way of gangbang denouement, before she leaned over the helm to slap the side of the boat, a trick to attract dolphins. I was beguiled, shocked when it worked. This is how I picture her at times, flanked by dolphins, white linen on white deck, cosmically at ease with her own fortune.

The "clay guy," whose name is Varesh but to whom Lark will continue to refer as the "clay guy," passes the test, predominantly by being nearly as charming as Sai. There is a great deal of forearm touching and laughter as they review various samples of clay. Lark believes herself to be an impeccable judge of character, and of clay. She has been ripped off numerous times.

They settle on a natural gray-gold variant, a terracotta hybrid, and the way the clay guy keeps referencing the spectacular beauty of the dunes of the Thar Desert, just west of majestic Rajasthan, without explicitly saying that this is where the clay has been sourced, you can tell he bought it online. Lark delicately trails her fingertips over the sample, testing the texture and color against the sun jutting through a slatted skylight. "It's perfect," she says.

On the drive back toward Haveli Dharampura, Sai takes a short-cut through a settlement comprised of scattered brick and concrete structures, splashes of paint on the walls and laundry strung above the road. He works the horn with staccato precision, jarring cyclists and pedestrians to one side of the road or the other, while Rishi obediently continues to play.

A handful of women look up from their work. Hauling, washing, selling, building, cooking, hustling. One has to imagine what one of these women would do had she been born into wealth. If someone had just handed her money. It isn't until Lark turns back to look at me that I realize I've said this aloud.

"Do it," Lark says, perfectly calm, her expression a dare. "Just hand her money."

I look out the window, and there are a lot of *her*s. "Who?"

"Does it matter?"

I understand that Lark's trying to make a point, but then, abruptly, there's a one-hundred-dollar bill in her hand, fished from the caviar leather Chanel coin purse she uses when she wants to appear grounded.

"Go ahead," she says. "Pick someone."

I don't touch the bill. I smile, instead, like she's made a cunning joke. "The distribution of wealth is already a little too stochastic for my taste."

She slides the bill between my fingers. "Isn't it better for someone to have it? It'll mean more to her than to us."

Lark asks Sai to pull over the car. Outside the window, several people have stopped to look. Rishi continues to play, his sitar scaling an atonal crest and descending, oblivious. "I'd really rather not."

"Okay, we'll go back to the hotel. Everyone stays poor today."

"Wait."

I look out the window and try to choose someone. There's no telling who's better or worse off, who's the most virtuous, most generous, who has the most children, the best idea for a startup, the smallest living quarters, or the most sinister disease. Who's having the worst day. Whose kid could write her own ticket if only the college application fees could be secured.

Before clutching and pressing the door handle, I try to do the thing Lark claims to do, getting a "sense for someone," scouring the features for lines that might mean benevolence or malice. I get out of the car and quietly move toward a woman in a blue sari, a skittish child curled against the slippery blue fabric at her thigh, and hand her the bill. I try to be subtle but am too obvious. There's no way not to be. The entire street has turned to watch. Everyone has seen.

It's clear now that I've coronated a target, if not of theft then of envy. The woman's face is only partly visible, but her eyes flicker with thrill and panic, a look not unlike game being hunted.

I get back in the car, where Rishi's sitar has picked up pace. "See?" says Lark. Outside the window, other women soberly stare, unchosen.

I haven't just given a person one hundred dollars. I've given hundreds of people nothing.

Over the course of my tenure with Lark, I've often pretended to be her. Sometimes it's an art world Cyrano de Bergerac stunt, a phone interview or email to a dealer, a rescue attempt from her signature vacillation between flirting and bullying. Other times it's to book tickets or lodge a complaint, to protect her from the anxiety of being on hold, of talking to people she can't see, or because I have all the numbers memorized and she doesn't.

That night, over martinis in the hotel lounge, Lark announces a new interview. I wonder whether I've invited this, her tendency to ask me something after a drink, or if it's a maneuver that predates me. "It's a newish art magazine, London-based, super-chic aesthetics," she says.

"Alright," I say.

The interviewer (Ben) is young, self-possessed but with a tight, nervous laugh. You can hear him shuffling hardcopy notes over the speakerphone.

As Lark, the directives are to be breezy, cool, smart but not too academic. Witty but not corny. If you don't like a question, just say something else. You're an artist, after all.

The last time you did a phone interview on her behalf, she sat across the drafting desk and mouthed things, her lips wide with exaggerated shapes you couldn't possibly hope to interpret as words, let alone articulable suggestions, and when you hung up she yelled, "Why didn't you mention the post-Anthropocene!?," which seems to have been the one expression from that Donna Haraway article that stuck, and you said it was because it didn't pertain to the work at hand, and just when it seemed like she was about to flip the table with eight different cyan oil paints or fire you or hire someone to break your kneecaps in the night, the magazine wound up gravitating toward the wrong quotes after all, printed the wrong things anyway, and basically just supremely failed to understand her work in all its complexity and contemporary relevance, and this, at least, was not your fault.

This time, the questions are all softballs. "I saw something on your Instagram about a secret project in Jammu and Kashmir. Can you say anything about that?"

"I'll just say this"—Lark loves it when you say "I'll just say this"—"There's no way to create art that's situated in both nature and civilization without aggressively inviting the post-Anthropocene."

Three questions later, when Ben expresses his gratitude and clicks off, Lark is already handing you a glass of champagne. She gives you a theatrical kiss on the forehead, leaving an imprint you'll see later like a ghost in the mirror, a lanceolate of lipstick the exact same color as her natural lips. "Fuck Europe," she says. "Those fuckers'll love this."

After champagne, a miniature compact appears—vintage, Chinese cloisonné—with a wad of what looks like ossified gum inside. "Live a little," she says.

You will never try heroin outside of Lark. So you say yes.

The minute it hits your lungs, you get it. You're a fan. You understand perfectly why people do heroin. The world is fists unfurled, languid with welcome.

Lark is jaded, more experienced, lazy with bliss. "Do you remember that night at Basel, when we did molly?"

"After Versace."

"Yes! You remember."

"I remember, but I didn't do molly."

"Yes you did. We both did."

"I didn't. I drank the Blue Lagoon you ordered, because you don't believe in drinking blue, which I fully respect, and then we got to the airport right before our flight."

"But you did molly."

"No."

Lark smiles a vicious smile, looks at you like you're lying, like you're a prude, despite the fact that you've just smoked heroin in front of her. "Okay."

"I didn't."

"Okay."

Lark smokes again. You take the pipe and pretend, already lush with regret.

"We did good tonight," she says.

"Yes," I say. "Yes we did."

In the morning, sunlight slathers the courtyard in a slick, soberly green-white sheen. Lark is already gone, presumably off haranguing the clay guy about the shape of the clitoris. I drag myself to the balcony, wishing for death. My hair smells like black tea and vinegar and, with a crest of nausea, I am decisively disenchanted with heroin.

Beyond the rollickingly hazy night of half sleep, dreams of granular gray-gold sand in my teeth and eyelids, the feeling of apathy but certainty that I've left the garage door open despite the fact that I don't have a garage and, if I did, it would be eight thousand miles away and beyond the scope of the plastic thumbnail remote I also don't have, something else has gnawed me awake, something worse, something Ben said during the interview: "The border of Jammu and Kashmir and what?"

"And it's a surprise," I said, not understanding the question, spurred by Lark's guidance to create mystery when one is confused.

Now, down a rabbit hole of guessingly misspelled Google searches, I discover that I have a much, much bigger problem.

Jammu and Kashmir are not two places, as Lark believes, but one place. Worse, she believes these two separate places to be at war with one another. And worst of all, she thinks these two distinct, war-torn civilizations are in the middle of the desert, a desert intended to be a perfect visual match for the clay she's selected for the apotheotic, sixty-foot arc of the *Cunt Bodhisattva*.

All of this is my fault. I've been nodding so alacritously, from the advent of Lark's vision to the momentum of its evolution, that I have accidentally nodded at sand, at wilderness, at scribbles on maps less cartographically sound than the New World as a volcanic swampland riddled with dragons. I've nodded us into a shared fiction, a nonexistent border in a nonexistent landscape, patrolled by nonexistent armed guards, lush with the mirage of artistic triumph. This nod, I realize now, is something I've picked up from Lark: the nod of attentive, partial understanding, of trust in one's own confidence above all, of willing one's own rightness into existence, of sorting it out later.

Historically, Lark has chewed through assistants like gum. I've lasted the longest. This is evidence of strength, I've always thought, although plastic outlives oak. Fake things always last the longest.

I'll be fired. Sued, maybe. She's done it before. I'll be ousted from the industry in LA, a cautionary tale about giving your assistant every advantage, flying her to India even, only to be so cruelly and incompetently betrayed.

As I squelch back my gag reflex and study the map for any hope of a tenable lie, a figure appears on the adjacent balcony, outside Lark's suite. It's Sai, wearing only a towel and a watch. He smiles, surprised but unashamed. "Good morning."

"Morning."

Sai has brought a small tin with him onto the balcony. He cracks it open, retrieves a thin sheaf of rolling papers and a wad of tobacco. As he prepares to roll a cigarette, he appraises me with genuine sympathy.

"Heroin?"

"Yeah. Heroin."

Sai sprinkles a bit of tobacco and weed into the right-angled crease of a rolling paper. He licks and presses it into a cylinder, then offers it to me, leaning over the cusp of the balcony. "It'll help with the hangover."

"Is that true?"

Sai shrugs. I lean out over the gap between the balconies, meeting him halfway, so he can light the cigarette.

"Something else, yeah? Worse than heroin?"

I have no reason to trust Sai. He is a half stranger in a persimmon-colored towel on my employer's balcony. Nonetheless:

"I've made a massive mistake, Sai."

I tell Sai everything. He nods with the quiet, seasoned calm of a detective who's just learned the truth, neither predicted nor farfetched. He lights a second cigarette, and when his phone rings, he answers it with one hand, smoking with the other. The conversation, in crisp Hindi, is liltingly familiar, curt.

"More H?" I ask when he hangs up.

He sets the phone on the small table beside his cigarette kit. "Don't call it 'H.' Makes you sound like a tourist."

"Lark calls it 'H.'"

Sai waves his cigarette in a gesture that says, well there you have it. "And no. That was my boyfriend."

"Oh." There's no graceful way to convey my curiosity or delight, or there is and I'm too hungover to achieve it, so I say, "I didn't know you were bi. Or pan or—whatever; I didn't know you had a boyfriend." It's the overloud tone of perplexed support I remember from my own youth, from parishioners who thought themselves hip, and I wince.

"I'm gay." Sai grins and smokes, pumping the cigarette between his lips as though he's fellating it, and also so that I can see the face of his new watch: a Chanel J12 with a quilted blue band.

"So Lark . . . ?"

Sai shrugs. "Which part of you is sacred?"

We smoke in silence, watching as more shadows move through doorways across the courtyard. I feel a surge of envy at Sai's ease. "Still. Don't get too excited."

"About what?"

"About that watch. Her Chanel gifts are never real."

Sai rolls another pair of cigarettes, then tucks them both between his lips and lights them at once. He hands one across the rift between the balconies.

"I'll help you," he says. "We can drive out to Hikkim, through the Spiti Valley. There's a route where the signs are all in Devanagari. She won't know the difference."

I nearly ask him why he's helping, but he seems to sense this already. "People like you and me," he says, "we have to stick together. For as long as it takes."

"How long is that?"

"Until we're them."

The following days are a slur of color and sound: the gumdrop-stained glass of Alsisar Mahal, the sunken gray riverbanks of the Yamuna River, swollen with hyacinth. Beneath everything, the tremulous lilt of Rishi's sitar.

It's difficult, in these days, to say what is and is not the real India. The raucous commerce of the Mochpura Bazar is the real India. The postcolonial wainscoting of the Surajgarh Fort is not the real India. Camels are the real India. Camel jerky sold at the entrance of the Mochpura Bazar is not the real India.

At nights, Sai and I drink ourselves into a state of ego, guessing (always underguessing) how often the bartender (who looks nothing like Dev Patel) will be likened to Dev Patel by a revolving contingent of white female tourists.

As the connective tissue of the operation, Sai has arranged with Varesh to transport the statue to the coordinates we've selected near Hikkim. Varesh, who's grown weary of Lark's impatient, overenunciated demand for the shape of the knees to "create more feeling," is more than on board. None of the eight drivers care, and all are loyal to Varesh.

We, meanwhile, are wending our way along a slightly more tortuous route to the west, a careful itinerary with the semblance of spontaneity —ancient temples and markets, pit stops for chai—half-built from Lark's memories, honed by Yelp reviews. The route is partly intended to disorient Lark, but Sai is right: between the sex and inscrutable signage,

Lark has no idea where we are. By the time we arrive at what she believes to be the border between Jammu and Kashmir, the hired crew will have already unloaded the interlocking parts of the *Cunt Bodhisattva* and pieced them together in the spectacular sixty-foot arch she envisioned. Photos will be snapped, a short video will be made, and Lark, clad in the white mousseline linen Fendi dress she's brought specifically for the occasion, will bow in the sand and worship the idol of her own creation.

This, of course, is not exactly how it goes.

North of Kaza, in the skittish, half-quiet hours before sunrise, we barrel east along the jagged lightning bolt of an unnamed road. Sai drives with both hands on the wheel, more focused than I've ever seen him. Lark bounces in the passenger seat, a vintage Leica slung around her neck, raring to capitalize on the magic hour. Rishi, who has tried to make conversation once or twice over the past week, has apparently accepted that this is not the role in which Lark has cast him, and now plays a persistent, hypnotic melody that quavers grimly each time we hit a dip in the road. I sit beside him in the back, dodging the neck of the sitar, watching each crest and hairpin turn the way one might wait for a tornado to finally touch ground. My only job on this leg of the journey is to distract Lark with conversation as we near the Dhar Lung Wooh Statue Point, the one landmark she might try to google when this is all over.

At last, the ruddy slopes on either side of the road give way to an expanse of cold desert, freckled with grass, gapingly empty beneath the sky. Threads of pink have just begun to claw up from the horizon like blood in a pool, casting a reddish glow against a massive, sinewy form towering six stories high: the *Cunt Bodhisattva* in all her glory.

Lark leaps from the car, giddy with her own magnificence. She runs toward the statue, beckoning me to record her running toward the statue.

Through the lens of the small camera we've brought, she looks like a ghost, her dress and skin both nearly translucent. She races beneath the arched back of the statue, then mimics its pose like a tourist.

Sai gets out of the car and stretches, flashing a thumbs-up toward

Lark. He checks the face of his knockoff Chanel watch, then angles it in my direction. 5:18.

He winks. We've done it.

Rishi hangs back, plucks a few final notes, then stops. The valley is silent.

"Where are the guards?" Lark calls.

"Further east!" I shout back. "This section of the border is clear."

Lark nods. She looks around like someone who has loudly declared for months that she doesn't want a surprise party, who is now disappointed that there isn't one.

When she jogs back toward the car, I realize for the first time that she's barefoot. There's a pair of sandals in the go kit, but she refuses. They won't look right in the photos. In ten minutes, her feet will be bleeding all over the place, but that's fine. It'll become part of the art, somehow.

As the sun rises, each detail of the statue emerges with the drama of a freshly discovered ruin. The crew Lark hired finished their work during the night, just a few hours ago, but it looks as though it's been here for eons. The nth wonder of the world.

Sai pops the trunk and extracts four flutes and a bottle of '02 Pérignon. I once made the error of not properly observing some guerrilla exhibit—a wheatpasting fiasco in Portland—and have always budgeted for this moment since. The cork is popped. The glasses are poured.

Lark untangles the strap of the Leica from her hair and snaps photos from every angle: the perfect curvature of the Bodhisattva's toes, the soft gaze of her barely open eyes. The meticulous rift of the ass and the V-like crease of the thighs like a strap on either side. The subtly sculpted rings of the throat.

Lark stares down the neck of the viewfinder, then smiles. She makes her way back to the car, where she leads us all—even Rishi—in a sloppily joyful, sleep-deprived toast.

As the sun continues to rise, tipping now from the magic hour to something less magical, a new revelation unfolds:

The clay, which in this light has the look of gold covered in dust, has begun to crack. Varesh has coated it in something, a sealant or epoxy of some kind, and when the sun hits it, the sheen of plasticky gloss begins to melt, slurring over the details of the statue. The cuticles of the toes dissolve, flattening the Bodhisattva's feet into what look like beveled fins. The same phenomenon takes her fingers, above which the beaded rings of carved jewelry have begun to drip down the vertical spires of her wrists and forearms. It's impossible to see from this angle, but I imagine the fragile comma of her belly button caving in a widening, hollowing swell, like a meteor impact in slow motion. The curve of her upper lip (closer to the earth, on account of her backward bend), painstakingly etched by some anonymous art student to convey a Mona Lisa smirk by way of Ishtar, dips and leaks toward the nostrils of her aquiline nose, which itself has drawn a seam between the molten divots of her eyes. Her tits by now are nebulous slumps, shifting the way patches of lava might, though not at the same rate, the perk of one nipple treading water while the other vanishes toward a dislocated clavicle. At the same latitude but the opposite side of the statue, the clitoris—lest we forget, the size of a basketball—has slipped from beneath its protective hood toward the underwhelming dip of the anus. Each labium has merged with the other labia; the majora/minora hierarchy has been fully dissolved. The focal cunt, of eponymic primacy, has slid into a glut of malformed clay and grainy silicon.

Lark's gaze, white-hot with adrenaline, already pulses with what will be a spectacular lawsuit, despite the fact that, as far as she knows, we're committing an act of vandalism on contested land. "It's the wrong clay," she says simply, each syllable a bullet of self-righteousness.

"It's the clay you chose," I say, and the minute it's out of my mouth, I know I'll be fired. Worse than fired, I'll fall within the concentric cancer of whatever legal action she devises. I'll be one of those trees that rips at the root before the local news has even announced a storm warning.

When the first of the legs snaps, the other pieces crumple in surprising sequence, half cracked, half resilient, tethered together with the inelegance of yolky meringue. Here and there the epoxy clings to a tendril of wire, like a sack of skin in which all the bones have been broken. Someone, somewhere along the way, fucked up, and this error became the foundation for another error, then another and another.

In the end, there will be only the wires left: stalwart and mortified as the masonry left after a nuclear test. A suggestion of something else: a city built for the purpose of being destroyed.

Lark won't have to fire you; you'll agree on it together. You'll call the airline, one last time before she changes the numbers, to move up your flight.

You'll meet other Larks. There will be Sylvie, then Ava J, then Branwen. Each will take something from you and leave something else in its place. With each apple will come a bit more knowledge of your nakedness, a bit more comfort with leaving the garden. You'll start to meet her everywhere, but mostly she'll live in the voice you hear come out of your mouth sometimes, when you're tired and a server leaves your water glass empty, or when a valet doesn't reset your seats to their original position. You'll be free, but there will always be a shred of you in the timbre of tight skin and good cars, the tone of voice that sounds like money. You'll be alright, better than alright. But it'll be like a virus, treated but not gone.

When Sai's car is stopped at a checkpoint—Lark's not a monster; he's driving you all back to Delhi, underscored by Rishi's increasingly reluctant score—a guard asks your purpose for visiting India.

"Just to see it," I say.

The guard sweeps both arms outward, boredly grandiose, as if to say: here it is.

It's only land, as it's always been. Ambivalent dirt, rocks that have no idea where they are. Lark is exhausted by the checkpoint but pleased by the advent of Wi-Fi, scouring apps, scouting the next big thing. Because I'm free and sad and unmoored and have always wondered and the stakes are low, I ask, "Is this the real India?"

From the front seat, although it will certainly cost him dearly, Sai laughs, then the guard laughs, and although Rishi doesn't laugh, he stops playing, and together they cannot stop laughing.

Obscure Trivia of the Antarctic

MARTA IS GOING on a trip. She has been asked (ordered) not to leave town, so she has decided to travel as far from town as possible. She has consulted the atlas, reverently traced her finger over the tendrils of longitude, dredged up the last of the undiscovered credit cards (the odd one, which since the onset has believed her name to be Marga), and booked a trip to that most famous of inhospitable and covetably remote destinations: Antarctica.

In her days of quiet planning, she pieces together the excursion like a quilt—Minneapolis to Miami, Miami to Bogotá, Bogotá to Santiago, Santiago to Punta Arenas—a stitching together of backwoods regional tarmacs. For a small (significant) increase on the already outlandish sum she's issued to Aventura Regia, she's elected to fly privately, cleverly avoiding major airports.

The trip represents all her money, which a doughy Minnesota prosecutor will one day prove, with unnecessary Grisham-like theatrics, is not actually her money. But the world is strange and unjust, and on the day she was denied an account at the very bank headquarters at which she worked, having functioned for so long as a grateful, invisible force presumed too stupid to record the account numbers left lying openly on the CEO's desk—numbers that were even then ignored, recovered only when the CEO had discarded that Post-it in the wastebasket it was her job to empty; even as he called her Maria, which is not her name—something switched inside her. An evolution of ethics, perhaps. Or a devolution. In any case, a shift.

The trip is unlike her, but her plans unfold with an out-of-character ease.

Of course, everything is normal once it's happening.

The night before the trip, she is sick with the thrill of it. Even as Angie trounces around the bedroom, ripping clothes from the suitcase and jamming them back into drawers, her stomach churns with a version of glee. Even as Angie swears, apoplectic, puzzling over the mukluks and the bikini Marta has planted as a diversion, ripping the toothbrush from its plastic travel case and hurling the pieces in opposite directions, Marta is unperturbed. Even as Angie crawls across their bed, viciously clawing the air and then Marta's shoulders and throat, Marta is sure. She has never been more sure of anything in her life.

Marta has flown first class just once before, the result of a plane crash thousands of miles away. Someplace off the coast of Europe, the same type of plane on the same airline had tumbled into the Atlantic, killing everyone on board, and passengers on this discomfitingly similar plane on the opposite side of the earth had fled. Marta, fourteenth in line for an upgrade, had been bumped up to seat 2A, like the secretary of agriculture ascending to the presidency during an apocalypse.

She had been nervous, charmed by the little flourishes—more cloth, more glass, better ice cubes, the basket of complimentary rolls presented with inordinate fanfare—but surprised by the lapses into normal air travel. Plastic cups during takeoff, the ceremoniously touted steak option nonetheless a glorified TV dinner. From her vantage point in 2A, she had watched the code-switching flight attendants slipping between first and business toward coach, the reflexive segues from doting servants to school bus chaperones. The of-course-sirs reframed as annoyance at requests for a lime, the sighing tutorials on the overhead air-conditioning spigots.

She had sipped her rum and soda, built on the finest ice available at thirty thousand feet, with an admixture of guilt and delight. She had felt like Eve in the garden, knowing more than was previously known, hating her sweatshirt, concurrently enlightened and rife with shame.

She had traveled since, but had never attempted an upgrade. It had ultimately been both marvelous and regular, a dalliance predicated on disaster.

Now, fifteen thousand feet above the Southern Ocean, Marta watches as the continent unfurls like a spilled bag of Domino sugar. Slopes of strikingly, savagely white ice appear, slashed through with rivulets of blue and gray. In a tone of rehearsed triumph, the captain announces that they are approaching Antarctica.

It has been a turbulent flight, and the floor is sticky with a sheen of spilled champagne. For the past twenty minutes or so, Marta has been listening patiently as a scruff-jawed game-hunter-turned-environmental-activist recounts his old life with the alacrity of a born-again Satanist describing his conversion. He is recalling, with a detectable vestige of delight, the strangeness of how a creature behaves when it's about to be killed. "Not just the trite violence of the proverbial cornered animal," he's saying, his mild brogue wet with Dom Pérignon, "but also the playing dead, the tricks, the weird little sounds, the antics." He leans close—closer, Marta thinks, than is altogether necessary to overcome the engine noise—and says, "In these final moments, an animal will act against its nature." Marta waxenly smiles and nods, courteously indifferent. She knows.

Marta is one of nine passengers: two smugly solvent Paris-based photographers; an erstwhile music producer/wearer of bracelets; the curator of a well-known New York gallery; the expertly plastic-surgered designer of something called "eco-sleepwear," accompanied by her husband, the dopily amenable CEO of a company whose purpose is undecipherable; a semi-famous author whose failure to produce any recent new work has been publicly attributed to his "always-a-bridesmaid" resentment toward the National Book Award; the aforementioned hunter-turned-activist; and Marta. When someone asks what she does, she freezes, then laughs and says, "Who can remember?" They laugh too, and she is presumed to be retired.

When the captain makes his announcement, the passengers stop chatting and press themselves against the oval windows, viewing the majestic continent swelling below through the lenses of cameras and phones. Only Marta and, to her surprise, the curator are empty-handed. They glance away from the sun-slick windows and share a look of inadvertent camaraderie, standoffish and bemused, as though they'd buried a body together.

The camp itself is a minor Eden. Individual pods litter a crater of snow and ice, flanked by a semicircle of cliffs on one side and the ocean on the other. Each pod is its own inviolable, eighty-square-foot fortress, a careful blend of futurism and familiarity. Fox furs draped over bannisters, espresso machines nested beneath wall-mounted heaters. Luxurious flourishes tempered by practical considerations.

Marta is no stranger to luxury, even outside her years of servitude. She has saved up for vacations, has bought the crackers that are not on sale. But never before has she disembarked from a DC-3 Basler and plodded through a veil of spun-sugar snow, swirling up from the ground like so many ghosts, toward a private little kingdom that is solely hers. Never before has she felt, from this angle, the exhilarant buzz of invasion.

Inside her little pod, Marta strips off her bloated, bright orange coat and hangs it on the hook by the door. She takes off her blocky snow boots and sets them neatly on the mat beneath the coat. She explores the room, its metals and woods, transplanted touches of nature, redolent of lofty mid-city hotels. She empties her pockets, just a tube of lip balm and the neatly folded ten-dollar bill she has carefully allotted for tipping, but there is no service staff in sight. Her luggage has simply appeared, by magic, presumably during the fifteen-minute orientation at reception.

She collapses onto a bed of furs and wools, 1,200-thread-count sheets. She takes a shower and is stunned by its heat, but chastened by a polite sign advising keeping it to twenty minutes. The books, she finds, are crisp and unread. There is no Bible.

Their first night at camp, the travelers gather for dinner. The dining room is an opulent rotunda, lavish and pragmatic. An army of heaters and humidifiers, strategically spaced between bookcases and bar shelves, approximate the normalcy of the indoors. Deep-set windows line the walls, and splashes of pale, cloud-strewn sky are visible, thickly blurred through panels of reinforced glass. The sun will not set this week, merely drunkenly dipping toward the horizon at sporadic intervals before perking up again. It is technically evening and candles are lit, though the room is flooded with the pristine white-gold light of midday.

Marta sits at one of ten identical place settings, amid multiple wine glasses and the full splay of silverware variants—salad fork, dinner fork, dessert fork, et al.—her fingers trembling on her thigh. Everything is clean, outlandishly clean, but, as before, the service staff is either absent or invisible. The designer and CEO have already arrived, as have the author and curator. The photographers appear, chummily debating something in lilting French, and the producer and hunter arrive together, deliberating in English whether the camp aesthetics qualify as "Kubrickian."

At last, the guide, a chic, rugged anachronism, appears in the doorway, flecks of ice in his exquisitely trimmed beard. He looks—and will look, on each of his many appearances this week—as though he has sprung forth fully formed from a Patagonia ad. He grins and takes off his boots, leaving his coat and hat by the door and throwing his arms wide with a beatific smile, like a golden-age TV father returning from the office to his brood.

"Look at you all!" he exclaims. He makes his way around the table, shaking each traveler's hand, although they have seen each other just two hours earlier. Finally, having made his way around, he clasps his hands together and says, "You poor things, at the edge of the earth and sober as lambs." He lifts his hands and, bizarrely, with the bravado of a matador, claps them together twice.

From a narrow door, two men appear, both dressed in half aprons over slacks and cashmere sweaters. "Charles," announces the guide, "our preeminent chef. Do not fall in love with him." A light smattering of laughter. The guide turns toward the second man: "And Barney, his sous chef slash—more importantly—your bartender. Anytime you need a taste of the old world, to get sauced night or day, or to make a toast—there will be a lot to toast this week—he's your man."

The travelers nod and smile, enthusiasm incarnate, lightly applauding.

"And I, of course, am your guide, here to satisfy any other damn request that may arise." He hears himself say "damn" and adds: "Pardon my French." One of the Parisian photographers rolls her eyes. "Now, Barney here will be collecting your drink orders—we don't have *every-thing,* but we do have the *best*—so order well. You paid for it." More laughter.

Marta has begun to relax; has burrowed her palms into the lamb-skin pelt attached to her chair; has pondered, briefly, the ordering of a martini, but realizes she has come so far and would prefer to indulge in something she actually enjoys; has surged with childlike curiosity and delight at the sight of a bottle of Diplomatico No. 2 Barbet, a pro-hibitively costly rum about which she has always wondered, atop the bar; has watched her companions slouch and fidget, sightlines straying, even now, with the practice of casual wealth.

The music producer, seated to her right, compliments her drink order and engages her in a one-on-one toast of respect as it lands, lifting his own glass of Lagavulin, the first of several, sensing in her iceless and non-wine selection a comrade of sorts, and Marta feels, with untethered bliss, that she belongs.

During dinner, the guide encourages the travelers to share something personal about themselves, to expedite the bonding process.

The eco-sleepwear mogul learned how to play the flute as a child. She has since lapsed, but conveys this bit of trivia with inordinate pride.

Her husband, the CEO, is purportedly part Cherokee.

The producer has produced, in addition to music, no fewer than three gorgeous illegitimate children, thanks in part to the excruciating and lonely birthing experiences of three separate and shockingly high-profile women. He has, perhaps not unrelatedly, had upward of four glasses of scotch in an hour.

The activist, whose signature conversion experience has taken on a disconcertingly wistful edge, recounts his dark past with reference to—an exploit conveyed with some excitement—the felling of a polar bear in 2007. The guide, who has consumed a beer and a half, placidly notes that polar bears are only found in the Arctic, and the hunter-turned-activist, he points out, would have to have murdered a penguin in order to be presently geographically relevant.

"I'd never murder a penguin," says the hunter-turned-activist, rife with self-righteous dissent.

"I'm not saying you'd murder a penguin," says the guide, placing a muscular, companionate hand on his arm. "I'm only saying that penguins live in the Antarctic."

"Cold, still," says the hunter.

"Indeed," says the guide, then looks toward the group as though the two had, despite a glamorous political clash, shook hands at the end of the televised debate.

One photographer is an orphan; the other can touch her tongue to her nose.

Marta was her class valedictorian.

The curator, as it turns out, is secretly an artist. This comes as no surprise to Marta, who has been exposed, for a good long while, to the phenomenon of selection as ersatz creation.

The author opens his mouth to say what his expression suggests will be something very, very interesting—scandalous even—but then simply announces that he has two dogs. A spaniel and a Labrador.

Later, during the third course, the guide regales them with obscure trivia of the Antarctic. There are no time zones in Antarctica: everyone simply adheres to the time zone of their home country. There is no currency. There is an annual marathon, a lonely and occasionally fatal affair in which wealthy health junkies jog through the research centers while the researchers, presumably, watch through their double-thick windows and roll their eyes. There are weeks of night, and weeks of day, and these spans of yeses and noes pin the world to its edges, an egg-carton cushion of livable moderacy.

He touts the transhistorical glitz of extremis. Everything here is the oldest, the newest, the first, the final.

The next day, they are slated to abseil a nunatak, two terms Marta feverishly googles using the camp's improbable Wi-Fi. She discovers, with some relief, that the plan is to rappel down a cliff of ice.

The travelers are on board with this excursion to varying degrees. Eco-Sleepwear is performatively thrilled, whereas Photographer #2 is surlily stationed in view of the cliffs, devotedly immortalizing an abscess of ice and earth on film. Photographer #1 swings by, in full gear, to deliver an offhand barb, while the producer, disenchanted with third-party insights, is back at the pods, napping. The author is here, in rare form, focused and jovial, searching for the next big thing.

Marta is interested, but quite clear with the guide that she has not rock-climbed in the past. He calls her Liebchen, an absurdly dislocated affectation, and tells her she'll do great.

As Marta descends from the cliff, the nunatak, as it were, she sees beneath her millennia of undisrupted, unfettered snow. It sneaks onto

the ice, bleeds onto the sea, has no observable issue with its own tran-
sience. Seems to know it will be slaughtered and reborn.

She reaches the bottom, and is told, upbeatly, not to cry.

There is a tradition, says the guide, of burying a secret in the snow.
When the snow melts, the secret will have vanished.

Marta believes this to be nonsense, but she buries a secret just the
same.

She has begun to feel the deep, raucous guilt of being here; of theft;
of the small possibility that she could have skirted a prison sentence if
only she'd stayed behind, stayed safe, stayed within the realm of rea-
sonable, state-sanctioned behavior.

She buries her secret but imagines it not dissolving, rather calcifying,
an ossified artifact of acknowledged regret, an homage to error to be
discovered in centuries to come.

She has been speaking aloud, she realizes with embarrassment, in
Spanish.

She remembers, vividly, the images of paleolithic Venuses, dark and
fat, reframed with respect as "voluptuous" and "of the earth," a cura-
torial sleight of hand. She closes her secret in the earth, brushes off her
gloves, and goes looking for Barney.

"You are not alone," says Barney, pouring from two bottles at once like
a Dionysian high priest.

She asks how many black people have been here. He says two.

She asks how many brown people have been here. He says define
brown.

She drinks, whatever she likes, the erudite extravagances of
Diplimatico-on-Lagavulin-on-WhistlePig-on-Clase-Azul-on-Crystal-
Head-on-Don-Julio-1942.

She is drunk, and quickly.

· · ·

The following morning is the first and only time she sees a member of the otherwise unseen service staff. At the perpetually sunlit window above the door, a woman hops and waves. Marta rolls from her side to her belly, then, laboriously, to her back. The world jolts and spins. The woman enters, having gauged Marta's floundering as an invitation to entry.

"Forgive me, ma'am," says the woman. "The plane leaves in ten minutes."

"What plane?"

"The plane," says the woman, her spine curled in a lifelong gesture of apology. "To the pole."

Marta rallies her body, with stiff recalcitrance, to a sitting position. "Who are you?" she asks.

The woman seems to consider this, then says, "I'm Luisa. I'm here to wake you."

"I'm awake," says Marta. Then, because she hears how brutally abrupt this sounds, and because she is still a bit drunk, she adds, "and I'm happy to see you."

The plane ride is rough, and Marta's mandatory five-hundred-dollar windsuit is sloshed knee-down with champagne. The guide is blithering about wind conditions and temperature fluctuations, but all Marta can think is *Enough with the fucking champagne.*

They touch down on a slick white runway that appears, to Marta, to be indistinguishable from the surrounding earth. She is glancing around for a sickness bag, understanding how gauche this is, playing it as cool as she can, and then, with the abruptness of a skater's descent from a triple Lutz, it's over. The plane glides and jerks to a halt, carving twin scars in the ice. Marta languidly shoulders her weatherproof backpack, disguising her hangover as ennui. She wonders how often other people have done this.

The passengers disembark, shuffling down the glorified stepladder, as the whir of the propellers rattles and wanes. Before them, a landscape of colorless plains and low-lying concrete structures sprawls toward oblivion. The Midwest of the Antarctic.

They are ushered, swiftly, into one of the concrete structures, where they are offered a fluorescent-lit bounty of cheese and wine. Marta is amused and revulsed by the centricity of alcohol to all their appointments, as though being one of the few, privileged visitors to Antarctica required constant, mood-altering reminders.

They are encouraged to wander around. There is the bay of flags, flapping rectangles denoting the countries prodigious enough to have sent people here in the early 1900s, and the research facilities, denoting the countries that, somewhat more quietly, are prodigious enough to have people here now.

There is, above all, the hulking Amundsen-Scott South Pole Station, a brutalist brick of pragmatic architecture. It is interchangeably called the US South Pole Station, the guide explains, rattling off a fresh bout of polar facts, despite Amundsen and Scott having been Norwegian and British, respectively. The US, of course, is where the money comes from.

Marta is transfixed by the sign heralding the geographical South Pole, and asks the author if he might take her picture in front of it. He does. When he presents the viewfinder for her approval, she reads, with gutted amusement, Scott's quote above her left shoulder: "The Pole. Yes, but under very different circumstances from those expected." She realizes, with a kind of morbidity, that this image will live alongside her mugshot on the internet for eternity, each vying (among a very small cohort) for attention.

The travelers are treated to a brief tour of a small subset of the station, where they shake hands with researchers who look both mildly sickly and healthier than anyone Marta has ever met. She is impressed, more than anything, with the normalcy of this place. How anything can be made to be normal.

There is a little gift shop, and Marta buys two postcards: one for Angie and one for her mother. She imagines Angie at some Minneapolis

Christmas party, waving the postcard around like a prop, soliciting sympathy from half friends with electric melodrama, conjuring her wild, fucking *wild* ex-girlfriend who abandoned her for, of all places, the geographical South Pole. The second postcard is likely to be received and conveyed by a nurse, respectful yet curious, to the small but clean, green-painted room where the paint is peeling from the walls in strips no wider than a finger, revealing the pink layer of paint underneath, creating in its flecks and curls the impression of leaves peeled back from flowers. Marta's mother, self-described as Moses on Mt. Nebo, having delivered her daughter to (in) the promised land but forbidden from residing there, used to and thankful for the monthly checks with a heart scrawled in the memo line, will be surprised. She will place the postcard on the windowsill and tell everyone.

Marta and her companions are ushered into another of the small, low-lying buildings, and here, with gleeful formality, they form a line. They advance, one by one, toward a ruddy agent at a card table apparently erected for this specific purpose. The ritual smacks of the sacred, and of jail.

The eco-sleepwear entrepreneur goes first, and Marta can see that her passport has an impossible number of stamps, seemingly all of them. It resembles the back pages of a prom queen's yearbook, a crowded wonderland of ink at odd angles.

Her husband, next in line, receives his stamp with the solemnity of a Boy Scout receiving a badge.

Marta's passport is stamped, etched with that most covetable of stamps, and something inside her shivers and breaks. She holds this little thing—the proof—and her pulse thrums against the viscera beneath her stomach. It will be taken from her, surely, but today it is real.

She has read the memorable advice to be present, to be here, now, aggressively present, but she is lost, elsewhere, at the theater decades earlier, swarmed, in pitch-black, by the sensation of being underdressed. She feels this same fear now, of the lights coming back on, of being discovered, on a school trip, wearing a sundress taken from the thrift store donation bin to the opera.

. . .

That night, camp is made. More aptly, it appears like a quarter from behind the ear, presumably erected by the same unseeable forces that clear the dishes and set them out again, good as new. The little colony of bright orange tents juts upward from a sheen of snow and ice, illumined from within, like paper lanterns lit and released into the sky. A special occasion.

The author has jubilantly filched a bottle of Macallan 15 from the main camp, and a small party forms as if by reflex. Marta, still profoundly hungover, is reluctant to attend, but she does so anyway. There is something about the aloneness of this place, its expressionless indifference, the thought that if one died here she would become food for nothing, that bothers her, worse than the cold. So she plods across the snow in her bulky boots, expecting to see stars although she understands the solar science of the earth's tilt, for no other reason than that she is lonely and exhausted.

By the time she arrives, the bottle is half-drained and the travelers, huddled in the congested heat of the author's tent, have taken on the oddly giddy, unchaperoned edge of a summer camp game of truth-or-dare.

"It's not that bad," the hunter-turned-activist is saying, "killing certain animals."

"Then why'd you stop?" says the CEO.

"Which animals?" says the curator.

The hunter-turned-activist eyes them both, apparently deciding which question he'd prefer to answer, then turns toward the curator.

"Dogs," he says. "The world is lousy with dogs."

Marta sits on a zafu on the floor, placing her back against someone's knees. Her hair is played with, a gesture of absentminded affection, and when the bottle is passed Marta recognizes the dark violet nail polish of one of the photographers.

The guide, that very afternoon, had conveyed that the South Pole sits at over nine thousand feet elevation. There is a formula for this, the producer is saying, how alcohol is exacerbated by altitude, but the author has read an article in the *New York Times* debunking this. He says it's merely fatigue, the brain not getting as much oxygen as usual.

A second bottle materializes from nowhere and, with the ostensible blessing of the *New York Times*, is consumed. The guide is reconnecting with an old friend at the research station, and in his absence, a darker, less moderated version of the getting-to-know-you game unfolds.

The eco-sleepwear mogul goes first. In the muted, scar-tissue tone of a survivor of rape or war, she says: "I grew up poor."

"How poor?" someone asks, and it is only when the mogul turns and looks directly at her that Marta realizes that she, herself, has asked this question. There is an ensuing babbling, like the pressing of a bruise, about public school lunches and being unable to afford the flute, during which Marta sympathetically nods, but when the CEO reaches over and grips his wife's hand, as though to affirm her bravery, Marta laughs. She laughs and cannot stop laughing. The producer laughs because Marta is laughing, because she, too, drinks liquor without ice, and says to the mogul, in a timbre as close to admiration as he can muster, "But look at you now. Jesus, you've made it." The mogul softens; the CEO kisses her ear, and the game proceeds.

The hunter goes next. He keeps one head—a white tiger—as a reminder.

"Where?" asks Photographer #2.

"When?" asks the author.

"In Asia, when I was young."

"I meant where in your home; where do you keep the head," says Photographer #2.

"In the game room."

"How old are you?" says the author, palpably barbed, possibly in response to the hunter's aforementioned stance on dogs.

"Open season, is it?"

"I only ask because the last wild white tiger was killed in 1958." A silence ensues.

"You killed a tiger in captivity?" asks the sleepwear designer.

"It's a *ranch*," says the hunter. "They're bred, okay, and they live wild and free on a *ranch*. It's not like I walked up and shot it execution-style in the fucking head."

"Christ," says the author.

"It's a *reminder*. I was a different person then," says the hunter, his cheeks ruddy with heat. "My foundation has raised over two million dollars for animal rights."

The producer moves on. He had sex with a man once, in the context of a stone-sober threesome after the Golden Globes in 2003, with—he states the female name loudly and then the male name in a whisper, a famous name—and concludes: "I shit you not."

The CEO has no secrets. When pressed, he glances toward his wife, and the game moves on.

Photographer #1 has had three abortions; Photographer #2 is allergic to sesame seeds.

Marta is on the lam.

The secret comes tumbling out with remarkable ease, almost no effort whatsoever. Her companions listen, rapt, to the straightforward facts of the crime, her subsequent excursion, her inevitable, imminent arrest. She finishes, and does not hear the author's secret, nor the curator's. She does not remember trudging home through the shadowy white wedges of undulating snow. She falls asleep in her own tent, feeling fine, wondering who is mopping the champagne from the floor of the DC-3 Basler.

The next few days transpire with lightning vividity. The plane returns the travelers to the more dramatic, desirable real estate of the coast. They traverse a series of ice tunnels, electric blue, as though some god had plunged their fist in the earth and spread their fingers. Above ground, the penguins, a shimmering mass of black and white flecked with gold, are loud and smell like hell, appearing in numbers too massive to be cute. They are, nonetheless, admittedly majestic. The sun circles like a vulture. Marta hikes, eats, sleeps like the dead.

. . .

On the day before they are scheduled to depart, Marta wakes to the feeling of a person leaving the room. It may have been Luisa, but she cannot be sure. It may also have been no one.

There is a folded sheet of cardstock, an invitation, elegant and generic, on the end table beside the bookcase. It requests her presence in the dining hub posthaste.

When Marta arrives, she recognizes the trappings of an intervention: people sitting in what they imagine to be comfortable poses, as though for a photograph; the shifting glances; the ironic, nervous drinking.

"To be honest, Marta," the guide says with a sigh, a caring but exasperated camp counselor, "this has never happened before."

Someone has turned her in—there's no telling who—but Marta, of course, is responsible. She looks from eye to eye, some averted, some soft with feigned sympathy, the intervention having taken on the near-comical pastiche of a murder mystery. But she doesn't care who, not really. The betrayal has little bearing on her future: they are leaving tomorrow, and there is no temporary holding cell at the elite resort on the Antarctic coast. Accused though she is, she will eat the same food tonight, will sleep in the same bed, as the rich do.

In the morning, she finishes packing and walks toward the plane—the same plane, the only plane—a bastion of luxury en route to disaster. The flight back to Punta Arenas will be exactly like the flight to Antarctica, except that no one will engage her in conversation, and she will not be offered champagne.

She will be arrested the moment she disembarks. She is technically arrested now.

No fuss shall be made. She will serve her time, as anything is served, with invisible dignity.

Months later, on a taupe brick of a computer in a prison library, Marta reads about the curator's return to her artistic practice. A successful exhibition, belligerently staged at a rival gallery, comprised of thirty-six glittering, slide-slick, jagged white plaster icebergs sliced through with blue and gray. In graffiti across the floor of the gallery, wall to wall: THE FLOOR IS LAVA. The show is ascertained to be a sly instance of progressive ecological advocacy, and is a commercial triumph.

Marta recognizes in this, with a jab of distaste and respect, the brutal opportunism of displacement as luxury, is honored to have experienced the experience of a lifetime as reduction to trivia.

Some years in the future, as a condition of her parole, she will attend countless support groups, therapy sessions, innumerable getting-to-know-you affairs. She will be asked, often, to share an interesting fact about herself.

She will have visited the Antarctic.

Octopus

I.

Our first summer as princesses, we are ravaged by the heat. Already, even before the perspiration slithers from our glitter-slathered pores, so little of us is us, beneath the tulle and the spandex, the polyester and rayon, the baubles and the brightly colored faux hair, the galaktoboureko layering of unbreathable fabrics. We're touched up once an hour or so, our waterproof mascara slick with sweat, our lipstick creased from all that smiling. Our gloves are aired, waved around in front of one of the dust-thick industrial fans, and then slid back up our arms, over the elbows. Our tiaras are doctored for scuffs and set upright atop all that hair, lobster red and banana yellow, as hair might appear in a child's drawing.

We are, as anyone will tell you, living the dream.

The air is thick with the scent of sunscreen. Cherry lip gloss. The powdery nothing-smell of unscented deodorant. There's a break room beside the locker room, where kings can be seen eating tacos. Fairies swear at their boyfriends on cell phones. Villains study for the GED, legs crossed, beside their elaborate headpieces. The room is thunderous with the whir of ventilation, blowing so much dead air up and over and back where it came from, again and again.

The bus ride each morning is arguably the funniest part, as though one could get to paradise on a bus. How far it drops us from the entrance is the second funniest part. You getting that tattoo removed on account of the off-the-shoulder gown, and because the special makeup that conceals tattoos turned out not only to be radically expensive but also to dissipate almost instantly beneath the heat of a Florida sun and the smudges of a hundred hugs an hour is the third funniest part.

The bus ride home is the least funny part. Surrounded by people who look so tired from doing whatever they've done all day, I realize I've missed it, whatever it is. People flex their necks, rub their forearms. They've carried things, moved things. I hurt, too—I've been waving like a maniac, dodging blisters, bending at the waist—but I haven't shifted anything. I realize, on these rides home, that I've been away from the world as it moved forward, and in the time I was away, it learned something. That now it knows something I don't.

II.

Both of us having gotten in was quite the coup (you remember), especially after Jenna told us how hard it would be. *The quizzes,* she said (you remember), *and the smiling—Christ, the smiling,* she said. *You'll never survive.* But then again, Jenna was always a drama queen.

After Jenna told us what had worked for her, getting-in-wise, we applied together. We proofed one another's applications, sealed them, kissed the envelopes, and dropped them in the mailbox together.

Our first day was the same day, and we were ecstatic. We were stunned by all the steps it took to get here—the bus to the park, then the bus within the park, the golf cart and the on-foot tour, the literal steps. We were assigned lockers and regarded them like shrines.

When I see myself in my dress for the first time, I am shocked. It's something I'll always remember in the present tense, like an early birthday party or a car crash. It's a trick of the mirror, has to be, but I cannot believe how flat I look. I look exactly like her, this other, made-up person. I'll never get over this, not ever, how little I look like myself. How much I look like someone else has drawn me.

Halfway into our first day, knee-deep in paperwork and handwritten notes, buzzed off the heat and the fact of it all, we meet Nathan.

Nathan is a legend. Nathan, of recognizable last-name pedigree, is chiseled jaw and thick hair come to life. He is smile where you can't see the lines between the teeth. He is cheekbones. He is shapely brows above the piercing blue eyes of a Siberian husky. He is skin of an angel who fucked a deer. He is god.

We're getting oriented (you remember)—hands crossed, legs crossed, seated in folding chairs, so technically chair legs crossed as well—when Nathan arrives. There is shuffling in seats. There are murmurs. Only Tanesha, lithe limbs not crossed so much as coiled, laughs, but she is not, at this point, the most celebrated of princesses, so her reaction is perceived as a slight. The rest of us are in love.

"Welcome to the park," says Nathan, and in retrospect, it feels like a game hunter addressing prey, but we are, in this moment, elated to be prey. We've been chosen, as confirmed by our deep packets of W-2s, NDAs, and the just-now-distributed sexual harassment paperwork.

"You're icons," Nathan is saying. "Of grace. Of beauty."

No sound is made. You could hear a pin drop. A zipper unzip.

"Every little girl wants to be you."

Just beside me, you catch your breath.

"You're what makes us exceptional. You're the heartbeat. The blood flow."

There's a hierarchy to the theme park, and it's basically comparable to the kingdoms it's designed to emulate. But the princesses here are a rotating channel of well-behaved worker bees, interchangeable and eager. The queen bee, really, is the prince.

The proverbial prince has fewer lines, granted.

But it's his kingdom.

III.

At the center of the park there is an octopus. It's called the Octowhirl, and it delivers, essentially, exactly what the name suggests. It is constructed with eight tentacular arms, and at the end of each is a bucket that seats as many as six to eight people. These buckets spin and whirl, dip and rise with the motion of the central machine, which is crafted, naturally, to resemble an octopus.

Rides like these have always been your favorite—since middle school, even, I remember this—not only on account of the spinning but the *double* spinning, the meta-spinning, the spin within the spin.

I don't care much for rides like these; I'm too prone to motion sickness. My father (I learned years after the fact) would smash up a generic dimenhydrinate into my juice box on any car trip longer than ten minutes. But it wouldn't be fair to say that I hate the Octowhirl. The first few seconds are bliss: the catching of breath, the sudden, radical lightness and lift in the stomach. Like the first drink of a night that can't be remembered by the end.

IV.

By some minor miracle, the Fourth of July falls on a Tuesday, and we're both off. Kendra, who thinks she's hot shit after a semester at UCF, has persuaded her brother to rent a pontoon boat, so we head over to Cocoa Beach. We drive with the windows down, and I realize I haven't felt the air on my scalp like this in weeks.

When we arrive, Kendra makes fun of us for how much sunscreen we're wearing—it coats our skin like see-through nail polish, not quite invisible—and you explain that a sunburn is basically a death sentence in our profession. Kendra gets a kick out of this, our *profession*.

"It is," you say.

"I'll bet," says Kendra.

You double down, although it's clear that you're just cranky because it's hot and we couldn't find parking: "I'm not kidding. A girl got fired for a sunburn two weeks ago."

Kendra nods a grave, lazy nod.

"Alright, fuck off," you say, "like you don't do shit for your job. Like you didn't ditch your fucking nose ring and start saying 'Yes, sir' every five seconds to sell fucking fake-ass jewelry at the fucking mall."

At this, Kendra laughs like a monster. She finds this hilarious, for some reason, and you laugh too. We all laugh. Kendra's brother, across the boat, laughs, although that seems to be about something else. It doesn't matter; it's a beautiful day and we're all laughing, we're all young and alive and American and it's the Fourth of July.

You reach into the plastic Publix bag we've brought and pull out the bottle of rum we got on the way over. Kendra's brother seems wary, but his two friends seem impressed, and he's not about to be the guy who comes between a good time and the underage girls who have almost certainly been described as "Kendra's hot friends."

Plastic cups are produced. Shots are poured.

We sit on the back and dangle our legs in the water. We're wearing bikinis, but it's only after two shots and a round of coaxing that I take off my clothes. I want to hide, to slip into the water, but all I can think of is how toxic the water must be. Of people pissing into the mouths of oysters, and other people eating the oysters, and some of those people dying of *Vibrio vulnificus*, which we've heard about on the news, and of their families at the funerals saying what a tragedy it is, as though someone couldn't have just *not* shat in the Atlantic.

V.

She was never my favorite, the one I most resemble. But princesses are princesses. At $13.75 an hour, we are all equals.

Part of the job is watching the movie, over and over. Her life—this other life I'm leading—only lasts ninety minutes (more if you count the sequels and holiday specials), but it gets lived and relived in tiny, sporadic increments over forty hours a week, week after week.

If you're not familiar with the story, here's how it goes:

The protagonist grows up in a broken home. Widower father. Her mother died when she was young; her father is adoring and proud, frequently wrong, a wildcard. Oppressively protective. Occasionally endearing. Out of touch.

Her mother, being absent, is perfection.

Our girl grows up believing that she's destined for something greater. She daydreams. Sings. Divulges her fantasies of a better life to the family pet.

One day, some low-grade crisis flares up and she leaves. She's drawn forth as though by a string tethered to her gut, tugging her along by a pain that feels like purpose.

She couldn't have known what she was signing on for. We can't blame her for this.

She's in over her head. But don't worry: she'll emerge triumphant, vanquish her enemies, and transition, with great pomp and an extremely shiny dress, into adulthood.

Above all, she'll be defined by this journey. She'll find her feet. She'll move up in the world.

She'll become sovereign.

VI.

There's a magic to owning something. To having your name on the door.

This is what I'm thinking at the signing outside the planetarium, in part because Nathan's name is on the door—or rather Nathan's father's, or Nathan's father's father's name, all the same name, of course, ancient royalty by American standards—or because I'm signing all these posters and trinkets and novelty booklets with a name that isn't mine. Either way, it's hot as fuck and I've been smiling for six hours straight and the way the humidity lands it's like the liquid is crawling out of your skin only to realize its error and sneak back in, bloating and leaking.

Nathan approaches so casually that it almost seems to be accidental. He has an expression I've only seen on TV before this moment, as though he, too, is surprised to be this successful. This handsome.

"Hey, stranger," he says, and I realize, as he stands before me, that the crowd has parted for him. That the masses innately, collectively understand that he does not belong in lines.

"Hello," I say. *Hey*, of course, is forbidden when in costume, like gum or knowing who the Ramones are.

"What are you doing after this?"

"Ruling benevolently over a peaceful kingdom."

He smirks. Rakes his fingers through a patch of thick, dark hair. Nearby, a little girl wearing a dress that matches mine hides behind her mother, watching intently, probably wondering which prince he is.

Because Nathan oversees personnel, and because his name is all over everything, he can go where he pleases. We princesses, on the other hand, have schedules that would make a chief of staff blush. Of course it's all waving and signing and dancing and hugging and the occasional parade, so when you say it out loud it sounds like we've done nothing all day.

"And after that?" he asks.

"Dinner, I guess."

"Come with me," he says. "After your . . . reign has ended. I'll pick you up by the waterfall."

And then he's off, trailed by the gazes of mothers and older sisters and a couple of openly gay princes, curiosity and lust following him like a royal train.

The remainder of the shift slogs past, mockingly slow, until the minute hand hits the twelve and I'm no longer a princess.

My stomach twists with the thrill of it. In the locker room, I sit in front of a vanity mirror, deciding. I wipe off some of the makeup, but not all, not wanting to erase whatever has prompted Nathan to invite me to dinner, in case this is part of it. I add touches of bronzer, of colors that aren't better or worse, only different, hues that look less like they belong in a drawing.

The air outside is thick with mosquitoes, crackling with cicadas, cool but heavy with salt and the sickly sweet scent of palm trees. Nathan is already parked, leaning against a spectacular steel-gray car, a little crown on the fender, just outside the private employee entrance alongside the waterfall. I had not known cars were allowed back here. Of course, there's no reason I would have.

Nathan opens the passenger door. Makes a theatrical, sweeping arm gesture. "Milady," he says.

I smile and approach, mimicking every girl I've ever seen in a movie where the romantic interest picks her up in a luxury car. Nathan grins and places a soft kiss on my cheek.

He adopts a jaunty tilt of the head. "Ready?" he says.

"Ready," I say.

"Brilliant."

In this moment, even as I get into a car more expensive than forty years of rent in my apartment, I feel something like a laugh fumbling against my rib cage, something like what Tanesha was suggesting at the coffee cart right after the orientation session, that the word "brilliant" is nonsense, that all of this is nonsense, that it will never hold up over time.

The steak place is basically a steak place, except that it's also the top floor of a ziggurat. We're in another section of the park, or more accurately another park within the family of parks, but at this height, in a plaster simulation of ancient Babylon, it feels like someplace else entirely. If you can get past the lack of regional specificity and the vaguely racist uniforms of the waitstaff, it's quite stunning.

We are treated like royalty. Wine is brought and poured. No IDs are checked. Aside from a delectable little prickle, a sudden lift and lightness in the stomach, nothing feels the least bit salacious about the presentation and pouring of the wine, the swirling and sipping, the smiling and consuming. That's the truth of it: if something is expensive enough, well-lit enough, established enough, and you're surrounded by people who are doing the same thing, it's almost impossible to think of it as a crime.

The evening—Nathan—is magic. The conversation is lilting, gymnastic. We laugh, fingers barely touching. At one point, he brushes the corner of my mouth with his thumb, visibly endeared, to rescue me from a crumb. There are candles, real ones, not the electric votives you see so often at restaurants closer to the ground.

I retreat to the restroom just once, to confirm the artful placement of lines and smears, a collection of optical tricks still in the spirit of a drawing, but one that's more my design than someone else's.

I return to the table, flexing my face and mouth against the new edits, and there is dessert. There are after-dinner drinks. There is prolonged eye contact.

As we exit the building, I stumble slightly on my heels, an aftershock of the amaro, a word I've only just learned, and probably also the crème brûlée, a term of which I've only just now learned the complex spelling, and Nathan catches me by the waist. He sets me upright. Looks into my eyes. His lips brush mine, apparently on impulse. He extracts himself, blushing, fishes for the valet ticket in his breast pocket. He stops, apparently struck by an idea. "Come here," he says. "I'd like to show you something."

Pressed against the base of the ziggurat, he guides me through a narrow service walkway. Hand in hand, we make our way through the dark. A minor adventure.

Behind the faux temple there's a lapse in architecture, an open space about three yards across. Local plants crawl the walls, a subtropic ivy of sorts, a small patch of wilderness amid a bastion of commercial intention.

"Marvelous, isn't it?" he says.

Left unattended, a series of thin, leafy branches has curled and pressed along the stones, then jutted toward the sky in a kind of slip-shod canopy. It is, in fact, marvelous.

Here, in the moonlight, his thick dark hair a bit tousled, shirt unbuttoned just enough to reveal the curve of his tanned, muscular chest, he looks like the cover of a romance novel. Like everything we've always been taught to love.

He lifts me by the waist and seats me on one of the lower stone tiers of the ziggurat. He steps forward, a palm flat on each of my legs, and insinuates his body between my knees.

"I want you," he says, and because I'm a little drunk and this is all a bit much, I laugh. *No shit*, I think. *I'm an icon of beauty and grace.*

He drags a finger along the crest of my cheekbone, the curve of my neck, my collarbone. His touch is alive with a fuzzy kind of delight. Pressed against my mouth, his skin smells like cedar, sandalwood, some impossible nowhere place that can be bought but not visited.

He bites the lobe of my ear, breath laced with spearmint and amaro, and whispers, "Do you consent?" I laugh, because this is a sentence I've never heard someone say before, and he repeats it, his tongue in my ear now, "Do you consent?" dancingly, almost as though it's a joke between us, a silly formality, a thing we've said before sex for decades, a private joke.

"Of course," I hear myself say, and then, as if by magic, my underwear is around my knees, his hands are everywhere, and this is what I wanted, of course, this is what I've wanted, forever, but it is fast and I am not so much a part of it as attached to it, along for the ride, alternatingly heightened and sickened, in the moment and eager for it to be over.

I've had sex before, of course, but it's always been between equals. I've never wondered how I was doing. Why I was invited.

He seems like a man who knows everything. He knows things about me that I didn't know, how to create sensations like a trick, to make me feel things, although *feel* is a funny word, how it can be part of you and not another part.

He says my name when he comes, and it's like part of my name will always be the way he's said it. When it's said aloud, there will always be a sliver of it in the sound of his voice. Like Adam naming the animals.

VII.

The thing I have always admired about octopi is their gift for disguise. Some octopi change color, enabling them to hide from their enemies. Others change color to match the environment so they can lie in wait for their prey. Between this and the squirming, the writhing, the wriggling through apertures no larger than your thumb, they are remarkable, slippery creatures in just about every respect.

I saw a story on the news about this octopus that escaped from its tank in a lab. It made it through the sewer system somehow, and got washed out of one of those drains beneath a curb during a flood. It swirled around for a few minutes, free as anything, before being hit by a car. According to the news, the driver had no idea what had happened until later, when he found suckers in the grooves of his tires.

From what I can tell, the Octowhirl possesses none of the magic or tragedy of the octopus.

We come here, one day, on one of our days off. Our families love the discounts. My father, an obese haze of bug spray; your shitty stepmom; a cavalcade of separate and shared children, all sticky somehow, all whining, all picking at their paper wristbands.

We board the Octowhirl, and you and I sit beside each other. Emma, one of your stepmom's kids, sits beside us, eating an ice cream cone like it's the last thing she'll ever do.

Once we're airborne, at the crest of the first whirl, I say, "I slept with Nathan."

"Slept with?" you say. "Fucked, you mean."

I look at Emma, but she's in her own world. "Yeah, fucked," I say.

The ride is picking up steam now, a swirl of activity spanning multiple planes. It's spectacular, the lightness in the belly.

If peripheral vision is to be trusted, you're eyeing me hard, with an expression both surprised and unfazed. "Behind the waterfall?"

"By the ziggurat."

Our plastic cart dips and swivels, plummets and spins. Children are screaming, everywhere. Where do children learn to scream like this?

"No shit," you say. "You too."

"No shit," I say, clutching the bar.

The ride ends. A glassy-eyed, polo-clad attendant unlatches the bar. He doesn't recognize us as princesses, since we're in regular clothes. As we disembark, Emma goes running in the direction of nowhere. I, to the surprise of no one, bend at the waist and vomit.

VIII.

One day, in the break room, I'm wearing a kind of poncho, a clear plastic sheath designed to protect my gown from pasta sauce. An older member of the staff—one of the doughily paternal widower kings— explains the allure of the Porsche 911. It is a casual car, he explains, one that you can as easily wear a t-shirt or a suit in. It's the sort of car you can drive every day. "It's not a Ferrari," he's saying. "People don't stare at you constantly on the road."

"But the 911," I suggest, "it's named for an emergency."

He stares at me like I'm crazy. As though I'm the Ferrari.

"You don't understand," he says.

"No," I say.

On the bus ride home, I am unrecognizable. I'm matted hair and naked face, L.E.I. jeans and Old Navy tee. You're somewhere else, on another bus, or in a car, maybe. Good for you.

In my lap is a tin-foil-wrapped meal, a well-meaning stab at waste not, want not, pilfered from the buffet.

We'll be back next summer. It'll be interesting. People do not age identically. Bodies form and fall apart in different ways. Give one cigarettes and another dairy or whatever and they age very differently. I've seen the studies. I've seen it happen.

When we're old, our smile lines will give us away. We'll have prematurely aged around the corners of our mouths and our eyes. How kindly we'll look.

If we're still friends then, and we're walking down the street or sitting someplace together, we'll look like all those queens in storybooks, regal and serene. People will see those ghosts of all those smiles and think: what a happy life they must have had.

Casualty

A MAN IS, BY ALL medical and anecdotal accounts, dying. He is suffering primary, secondary, and quaternary injuries including, but not limited to, pulmonary barotrauma, mesenteric shearing, and penetrating ballistic gastrointestinal perforation, which is to say that blood is leaking, syrup-thick, from his abdomen, fully destroying his Cambridge University T-shirt and the waistband of his pajama pants. As a British Panavia Tornado warplane careens overhead, the irony of his extraordinarily British alma mater is not lost on him.

He is scheduled to perform surgery in the morning, but somewhere along the erratic drive, the haphazardly lopsided parking, and the short, limping hike through rock-riddled sand, he has realized that he will not make it. On top of the splanchnic agony ripping through his body, he feels bad about this.

He has come here, to this low-lying well outside the city, with no agenda except that he does not want to die in the street. He does not want to die in his bed. He wants to die somewhere holy.

He sinks to the ground and slumps against the erratically sized stones, his medical bag braced between his knees. During his time in England, a charmed stint of polo shirts and promise, he learned that this, his home city of بغداد (Baghdad), once fell within the bounds of the Roman Empire. That this magnificent attempt at world domination sprawled all the way to the gulf, as did the subsequent invasion of Germanic tribes. That after scything their way through Europe, this illustrious batch of second-wave colonizers adhered to a peculiar tradition: they threw their enemies' weapons into a well. That this gesture was predicated on wünschen, the making of a wish. That it was also predicated on wähnen, an etymological collision of *imagination* and *to wrongly suppose*. That it represented a sacrifice to the gods of war.

Aman once wrote a paper on the contiguous inventions of daggers and scalpels, causes and cures. He is transfixed, even now, by the sacred disposal of weaponry, the wishings for luck. He imagines the water tasting like iron for decades.

With shaking hands, he fishes a wad of gauze from the bag. He locates a bottle of disinfectant, a needle and spool of wire. He bites down on a small emergency flashlight, tilting his chin toward his chest, and as he rolls up the edge of his Cambridge T-shirt, he begins to cry. The center of his body is a disaster, a wonderland of raggedly seeping and undetectable wounds.

The bag itself is a relic, gifted during the London bombing of Harrods in '83. Aman had been fantasizing all semester about winter break in Kensington, the guest room at his roommate's childhood home, a view of the park and shaking his accent once and for all. He'd been there for two days when the news struck, and his roommate's father—himself a doctor; they all seemed to be doctors—had rushed toward the hall closet and retrieved the bags. Aman and his roommate, both certified paramedics, had joined the doctor in the Rolls and sped toward Knightsbridge. The street had shimmered with glass, plaster, and ash like snowfall, the torsos and limbs of mannequins bizarrely strewn among the real bodies. It had been a blistering crash course in triage, and as Aman had moved from person to person, bewildered, conducting the brutal math of survival chances and suspected injuries, he'd understood that terror reveals what is always true: that lives are not worth the same as other lives. Not in times of crisis. Not ever. He'd ridden back to Kensington in silence with the bag in his lap, eager to return it to the hall closet, but the doctor had placed a hand on his shoulder and said, "Keep it."

In his medical practice, Aman has often gently pressed the wound following the application of the final stitch, not to swab up the blood, but to reassure the patient. "There," he has often said. "That's the worst of it."

He presses his own wound now, summoning the pain, wanting to live. This, he knows, in his rapidly hemorrhaging gut, is not the worst of it.

He will miss the surgery in the morning, the sunrise, the string of derivative aftermaths to the incisive glamor of Desert Storm: Desert Sabre, Desert Falcon, Desert Strike, Desert Fox. He will miss the report of somewhere between 100,000 and 200,000 civilian casualties, a margin of uncertainty almost comically imprecise for such precise bombs. He will miss his ten-year reunion, where an old college friend, now an RAF pilot, will remark on his curious absence, scotch in hand, following a slideshow on the valorous exploits of Cambridge's veteran alumni.

Aman finds a marker in the bag, the one used to notate statuses on triage tags. He uncaps it with his teeth, then shifts his weight and, with excruciating effort, pries a loose stone from the well. On this stone he writes, in English: HERE LIES AMAN. He reclines against the stone, like a pillow, the words directly above his head.

He imagines his body being discovered. "We found a man," he imagines someone saying, not understanding that this is his name—that he is not only *a man* but *Aman*, a name older than the well—meaning trust.

He is, even now, enthralled by the terminology of war: *operations* and *surgical strikes.* One by one, he pulls the tools from the bag and slides them over the top layer of stones into the well. A sacrifice.

Aman is bleeding now, aggressively, from everywhere. There is blood in his hands and the curve of his belly, throbbing in his ears, the scent of it in his nostrils and its dampness on its lips. His tongue is sheathed in blood, thick with the taste of iron.

Above the city, the sky is a parade, streaked with the festive, marmalade orange of bombs and tracer flares. From here it looks like a celebration. A tremendous success.

He is still waiting for the worst of it.

We all are.

Bottle Girl

AMY IS twenty-one today.

(Everyone is twenty-one today.)

The club—seafoam green, on the insistence of a long-since-vanquished investor—thrums with the buzz of a thousand bees. Bass as buzz. Flirtation as buzz. Crane-necked/half-verified celebrity as buzz. Neon sign reading EXCEPTION AS RULE, hot pink and glittering, as buzz.

Amy visited a bee farm once, in youth, on a middle school field trip. The bees were endless. A woman in a netted helmet pulled a full-on honeycomb out of a box. Amy had not realized, prior to this, that a honeycomb was a thing outside of cereal.

Mrs. Parker couldn't be blamed, of course. Twenty-eight children is a lot, and when two of the twenty-eight overturned a beehive while she was watching the other twenty-six, there was an eruption of screams. Bees were everywhere. Children scattered and fell like bullets from a sawed-off barrel. But Amy stood perfectly still. She'd been stung thirty times, the doctors said. Amy's mother was a livid wreck, suspicious of the round number thirty. She spat on the tile floor of Saint Francis Memorial and made it known.

All Amy remembers is the sound.

But the buzz was nothing compared to this.

There's another neon sign, in the ladies' room, that reads NATURE IS INVENTION. There are a thousand images on the web—Amy's seen a few of them—with women beneath the sign: lips malbec-red and bronze and coral and pretty-in-pink and blue and once really blue, though the last of these was resolved with an ambulance out the back and, later, a modest settlement.

Anyway, Amy is, as it turns out, allergic to bees.

The ceiling of the club is a lattice of pipes, all leading to nowhere. Technically, there's one pipe that matters, a fat ventilatory pipe, and someone—presumably the same ousted club investor with an affinity for seafoam green—had the bright idea to build a maze of thin nowhere-pipes, faux infrastructure-as-artwork, around it. The sound in the club drifts up and rockets around the pipes like a pinball, echoing back down as a tantrum of sound, a rearranged mist of inside jokes and pick-up lines descending damply below.

Amy slouches at the rail over section 4, half-lit by the vintage banker's lamp on the hostess stand. Viewed from below, she is one of eight silhouettes, each seeping into the other in an undulating caterpillar of hair and skin. If lit from the front, they'd look like a calendar from 1994, a strappy, inconvenient mass of breasts and hips mediated by hourglass middles. Latexy leather, delicate chains accentuating décolettés, metallic strings dripping between tits, glitter-laced lotion slick on the same collarbones over and over and over.

To Amy's right there are Mel, Elise, Indica (whose real name is Gladys, after her grandmother, but who's experienced a 26 percent increase in tips since opting for Indica), and Arielle. To her left are Iris, Lane, and Bérènice. This is the last moment of fidgeting, of sleepiness, of normalcy (costumes notwithstanding) before the door is broken down by the thrum that's already audible, little-black-dress-clad clubgoers and hedgefunders like orcs, hungry for the press of bodies and Belvedere, swan-shaped ice buckets and sparklers in the offing. Enthusiasm like a horizon leaking toward the doors.

"Happy birthday," says Indica.

And the party begins.

Beneath the canopy of superfluous piping is a crowd, whirring and eddying. Nestled at varying heights are the tables, geodelike slabs over zebra-skin rugs that everyone's pretty sure (but not completely sure) are fake.

Tonight it's the same crew of Germans from last week, give or take a couple, smacking one another and guffawing, their Stemar boots pressed flat on the floor, knees wide, oblivious to the angle of their own suit-clad crotches, slouched and electric with self-congratulation. There's a twenty-one-year-old birthday party, bankrolled by someone's father's last name, then the next. A table of athletes—basketball players, Amy is pretty sure, from their shape and the profusion of rare-edition Air Force Ones. That dimpled actor from that new show, network, who hasn't figured out how to spend the money yet. The Donner Party, which has to be a joke, except that it isn't. A handful of bachelorettes, faces and skin shellacked with wealth, their bodies painted with variants on the same lacquer-sheen dress in emerald, gold, sapphire blue, with straps in functionless configurations around the collar, leaving little indents revealing the extent of their tans.

At the table of athletes, Elise is seated in one of their laps, the second-to-main one. The main one is famously married, recently forced by a slew of magazine covers into a season of chastity, or at least a period in which girls who look like Elise don't publicly sit in his lap. There's a bet, to see if she can coax them into another $10K, and she'll win, though the causality of Elise's presence is strictly conjectural. There's always another $10K. When the spend lands, Amy helps Iris and Bérènice haul a Nebuchadnezzar of Cristal to the table. Sparklers crackle, casting a hazy, orange strobe of smoke and light, spectacular but contained, like the bombing of a distant village watched on TV.

The girls stay to serve the champagne, and are invited to help consume it. Amy sits on the arm of the slick leather sofa, one gangling leg draped over the other, an unrecognized hand resting lightly, politely on the small of her back.

Amy's always preferred the athletes, sensing in their entrances and exits an aura of inspection, as though they dipped in and out of existence when watched and unwatched. They belonged to the tightly assessing gazes, the guessings at strength and weight, the paper-doll conjectures of how they'd look in various poses, in and out of clothes. Graceful and drenched in magic. Mel tracks the news, business, and sports, and often gawks, half-lit by her phone screen, at the figures—who earned what, whose contract just got pushed to which mil—but Amy is unfazed. To be owned that way, she thinks, to belong so thoroughly to the long look and the calculating half smile, they deserve every penny.

The Donner Party, who turned out to be a team of lawyers, has ordered appetizers brought in from off-site. Amy helps Lane retrieve them from the back serving station, where they've been extracted from their nondescript delivery boxes and artfully plated. The china dishware is freckled with translucent pink droplets of blood. Steak tartare.

"Morons," says Lane, balancing a string of plates on her slender forearms, a holdover from a past life at a steak restaurant.

It's something, Amy thinks, *the circumstances under which eating blood is accepted.*

Following the childhood incident at Halford Honey Farms, Amy had become enthralled by bees. She'd checked books out from the library, squandered ink from the slow-moving Canon on color printouts of various species, URLs with *Apis koschevnikovi* and *Apis cerana* faint in the corners of the pages. She tucked the printouts and trivia, meticulously handwritten, into a folder, which she studied while her mother cooed over her, dabbing Neosporin in thirty places, wincing as though it were her own flesh.

Amy had learned—and announced, folded glumly in the empty tub—that the venom from a honey bee is more lethal than cobra venom by volume. That it's also used as a treatment for high blood pressure and arthritis.

Amy's mother was not listening, more concerned with the obviation of scars, propping a first aid booklet open with her knee on the bathroom tile.

"All worker bees are female. Did you know?" said Amy.

"Of course," said Amy's mother, although she didn't.

"They never sleep."

Amy's mother dabbed three buttons of hydrocortisone onto a trio of red lumps just above Amy's knee.

"The buzzing," said Amy, "it's their wings. Flapping over two hundred times a minute."

Amy's mother angled her neck beneath Amy's outstretched arm, slathering vitamin E on a patch of puckering skin near the armpit.

"They all died," said Amy.

"Who died?"

"The bees," said Amy. "When they stung me."

Her mother flinched at a particularly prominent sting, nestled in the skin between Amy's nose and mouth, which she seemed to instinctively know would leave a scar.

"Good," she said.

In the VIP lounge, a guest has insisted upon celebrating some event with dessert-based nyotaimori, and this request has apparently been indulged. A woman with cropped black bangs lies fully nude on a length of table, her body lined with truffles, blackberries, French silk chocolate shavings, dollops of mousse. Shards of brûlée like broken stained glass. Mini cheesecakes.

"It's your birthday?" Mel edges past the velour-roped stanchion, past Amy, with a tray of tittering champagne flutes. "Indica said."

"Yeah."

"Happy happy." Then: "Emilio's, after."

Amy nods and wavers at the entrance, a chilled bottle turning warm in her grip. Inside, a parade of suit-clad men hangs jocularly around the table, laughing in a tight spectrum of tenor bravado, making a show of ignoring the confection-strewn model, affecting ease. They perk up at the advent of glassware, of Mel. Someone they know what to do with.

Amy marvels at their unnecessary layers: suit jackets, ties, tie pins, pocket squares. She is herself a palate of minimalism, straps and strips of cloth, as little as possible.

In the course of most service professions, running into someone you know is inevitable. Tonight it's Kevin, a former classmate, one year ahead, the voice of the morning announcements in the same regime in which Amy served as student council vice president, a sinecure befitting her social rank at age twelve. He recognizes Amy before she recognizes him, which is to be expected. So much more of her is showing.

He catches her by the wrist and looks into her eyes. "You look fucking wild!" he announces, already loose. "You aged the hell out of your ugly duckling phase." Amy's heard it called that before, her "ugly duckling phase," but it had never been that. She had simply been tall and thin in a way that scared people.

Kevin is sweaty and wet-eyed, a doughier iteration of his middle school self. He's a doctor now, he's saying, though Amy has not asked.

"Of what?" she says.

"What of what?"

"A doctor of what?"

Kevin laughs. "Of *medicine*."

"What specifically?"

The table glows with mixers, ordered but untouched, lit from below and gleaming like traffic lights. Kevin swallows a mouthful of whiskey, his thick, pallid hand a hamburger bun around the glass.

"Podiatry," he says. Then, brutely: "No one dies on my table."

"Mine either."

Kevin laughs at this, loves this. "Fuck you," he says joshingly, then, "It's better money than you think."

"Good for you," she says, and from the shift in Kevin's expression, he must know that she makes what he makes.

Mel has been steered, gamely, toward the dessert table. A liaison of sorts. She is laughing, mouth ecstatically overwide, chin angled in poses of catalog flirtation. At the coaxing of the group, she bends at the waist, hands clasped behind her back, and eats a blackberry, nested in a dollop of whipped cream, from the model's ribcage. As she rights herself, tonguing her lips and laughing, there are hands on her arms and waist, knuckles riddled with hair, wrists heavy with watches.

A man gestures for Amy, and when he does, the champagne in his other hand sloshes over Mel's collarbone, drizzling over the curve of her chest toward the low angle of her push-up bra. He motions toward Mel with the ebullient theatrics of a gameshow host.

"Lick it off," he says.

Amy and Mel laugh, together, a flicker of eye contact conveying the humor of a dark inside joke. They're already in the car, on the way to somewhere else, counting the money.

With the fearful awe of a zoogoer, Kevin watches, glassy-eyed and enthralled, as Amy licks the champagne from Mel's breast.

"We knew each other in middle school," Amy hears Kevin say, his voice soggy and unmodulated, the wrong volume for the room. "Amy's a freak." The cohort laughs, variants of disbelief and you-lucky-dog, misinterpreting his gist. "She used to carry a two-liter bottle of Coke around school. With a bee in it." The laughter is loud, confused, writhing around the pipes and crashing back down like a mash of confetti.

Amy wants, in this moment, to drag her hand through the stripes of

custard, the freckles of nonpareils. She wants to dig pebble-hard sprinkles from beneath her nails. She wants to bite the strawberry straight
from the woman's mouth and not even eat the whole thing.

Over a weekend, after the scar above her mouth had only partly healed,
Amy had tracked down a patch of black-eyed Susans, which she had
swiftly ascertained to be a hangout for bees. She had read, in her exhaus-
tive research, that bees are attracted to caffeine, so she had arrived with
a nearly drained two-liter bottle of Coca-Cola, dark liquid splashing
around the four-leaf clover of plastic at the base. She had sat on the
ground and planted the bottle within the cluster of flowers as a trap.

There was no way of knowing how much time had passed, but when
a bee zoomed through the little portal of the bottleneck, Amy was
thrilled. She screwed on the cap and watched, mesmerized, as the bee
darted toward the pool of soda, proboscis outstretched, jointed legs
dipping in and out of wetness. She panicked, struck with the thought
that the bee might drown, and poured out the bulk of the soda, careful
not to let the bee escape, then hurried home, where she offered more
soda through a dropper, watchful and restrained.

She must have known the bee would die, but having seen how casual
bees were with their own lives, was undeterred.

She slept to the hum of its wings, better than any idling TV set, the
THWAP THWAP THWAP of its bullet of a body against the plastic.
She marveled at its fur, so like the down of a baby chick, the glossy bulbs
of its eyes. She wondered, fleetingly, whether it missed its hive or was
content with its solitary fortune.

On Monday, the bee was still alive, so she took the bottle to school.
This defined her for a little while, in the way that minor eccentricities
do. It was close enough to scientific experimentation that the teachers
allowed it. The bee lived for days, blitzed on a diet of high fructose corn
syrup, caramel color, phosphoric acid, and caffeine.

On Wednesday, in study hall, she watched it die, whirring and slam-
ming its body against the frame of the bottle, its wings invisible except

when motionless, etched by light and shadow, defined by external conditions alone. Someone hummed "Taps," making mouth sounds like a kazoo.

It died in a haze of ecstasy, she imagines, buzzed to oblivion, unaware of its own fate until the final instant.

Amy leaves the flaccid, uninhabited shape of her costume strung over a hanger on a rack populated by similar ghosts, all destined for dry-cleaning and resurrection. She sloughs off sections of makeup, replaces them. Borrows a lip color that doesn't remind her of anything. Puts on her own clothes. In the glow of the vanity mirrors, she looks resplendent, godlike even. Anyone would.

She crosses beneath a lesser member of the constellation of neon lights—YOU ARE ALIVE in foxfire green—at the service entrance, the outside world like a train that's left without her. She gets in a nondescript car, Mel's car, basic and black, its costs all auxiliary: parking, parking tickets, title, and insurance. The inside is lavish with odd touches: cherry-red Audi seat covers, although the car is not an Audi; vitamins like candy in the ashtray; a tampon, clean and frayed, dangling from the rearview mirror like a lucky rabbit's foot.

In the moment before Mel switches on the ignition, there's a rift of silence like the vacant racetrack of space between songs on a record. The radio kicks on and the moment is past.

Emilio's is more of a recurring party than a place, effervescent celebrations of nothing on a routine cadence. Emilio is often absent, which Amy suspects to be a half-witted attempt at Gatsbyesque mystique, although she's met Emilio, everyone has, so she's not sure what the point is.

She knows already what will happen at the party.

She'll meet someone. Someone who's *someone*. They'll drink something, smoke something. He'll recognize youth on her like a cloak, damp with the impulse to wring it out, knowing it won't last. The party will drink to her health, her birthday, as though they wouldn't drink otherwise. She'll circle back to a half joint on the roof. Will wake at his place after a half hour of sleep, tiptoe to the foyer (he has a foyer), where a series of portraits hang. The portraits are of royal pets. Greyhounds, Persian blues, a leopard. All staring dead-eyed into the camera. All tamed.

Her favorite photograph is of a bleak-looking bull terrier, Dotty, the dotted, uninventively named pet of Princess Anne of Edinburgh, accused of canicide and attempted puericide, who even in studio photography looks like it's plotting a murder. She imagines blood around the puckered pink of the snout, flecks of skin beneath the well-trimmed nails. Her second favorite is a series of Windsor goats, framed individually in the style of high school graduates or confirmands, each respectfully ovalled in mahogany, all in full military regalia. There is something at once farcical and noble about them, she thinks, posing effortlessly, outranking humans.

He—her date, presently half asleep at a wayward angle in his infinity-thread-count sheets—is important, she supposes. He is important for moments at a time, all the time, and if you string enough discrete packets together you get light. You get importance.

When he wakes up, dragging a Henley over his forgettable torso, there's something like guilt around him, like a stench. "You're so pretty," he says. "Beautiful."

"Thank you."

"I know a guy," he says, and the way he says it sounds like an apology. Like he'd like her to remember him fondly. "A photographer. He's good. *Really* good."

"Thanks." Amy is always thanking people.

The air hangs densely between them. There is breakfast and, at the doorway, a goodbye kiss mashed between the corners of their mouths, the angle of an avoidable car crash. Amy will call him in a day or two, committed to the bit. The pretense that they really like each other. That this is not just the things they have, reputation and youth, a one-for-one exchange.

...

Amy has read about Elizabeth Báthory de Ecsed, the Hungarian countess who lured young women from neighboring villages to work her estate, convinced she could stay young by bathing in their blood. In the winters, she would strip them naked and leave them in the fields to freeze. In the summers, she would strip them naked and drizzle them with honey from her own apiary, letting the insects eat their skin.

In the interstitial spaces, alongside the garment rack or at the back serving station, the girls talk about their futures. Iris is working on a lingerie line. Indica aims to invest in real estate. Bérènice will travel. Elise is going to NYU in the fall, although she may delay a semester with an eye toward paying for the whole thing up front. They talk about the money like it's money and nothing else, as though no other cost will have been exacted.

Amy wants only to be elsewhere. Just last week, when she came across a website featuring derelict castles for sale, she fell in love with a fifteenth-century fortress in the Lleida region of Spain, as tall and thin and impenetrable as any building she has ever seen. Although she does not and will never own this place, she arranges to have her mail forwarded there. Since all her bills and payments are electronic—she has not opened a piece of hardcopy mail in years—the stakes of this whim are low, but she delights in the thought of her credit card offers and coupons trekked up the cobblestone path. She is thrilled by the automated email: "Congratulations on your move!"

Amy only needs one day off from the club but requests three.

The photographer's studio is whiter than any room she's ever been in. There are needlessly exposed pipes tendrilling their way across the ceiling, and she feels at home.

"I love this," the photographer is saying. "I love it; it's madness." His thumb is on her chin, a finger stroking the half-dimpled skin at the crease between her nose and mouth. "Not quite a beauty mark, is it?" he's saying. His voice is fictional British, Yale British. "You were born with it?"

"It's not a beauty mark," says Amy. "It's a bee sting scar."

The man is deciding, clearly, whether this is more or less magical. He looks at her closely, then stalks toward the slick bay of lighting and camera equipment and yells something vile at the camera operator. Although they're out of earshot, Amy recognizes the squeamish certainty, the shrinking relief of knowing, at last, what someone expects of you.

It's all about the scar now, the photographer is saying. She can't hear him but she can tell. The way the lights are shifting, the puzzled, stoic loyalty of the makeup artist who re-dabs her face.

The whole story is the scar.

Ori Dreams of a Tree

FROM THIS FANTASTICAL HEIGHT, the world appears to carve itself into dissenting planes: a slick, thrumming quilt of asphalt rivulets and right-angled topography. Highways slither and pulse like veins, as alive as anything, curled around patches of green with the matter-of-fact hunger of snakes around mice.

Ori clambers onto the flower-patterned loveseat beside the window and presses her nose to the glass. From here, she can see everything. She cracks the window, ever so slightly, and tips out a droplet of water from the mouth of her lidded cup. Somewhere, a dizzying distance below, the droplet lands. She surges with the divine thrill of a god, having made rain.

She ventures below, of course, hand tucked in her mother's hand.

Her backpack, bumblebees dancing over grass, bounces against her small frame. As they pass the flat, construction-paper green of the local park, she looks up, as she always does, toward her home, from here just a rectangular fleck of glass among a million just like it, anonymous as a star amid its galaxy, reflecting the sky back to itself.

Today at school, the teacher announces with feigned glee, we are learning about trees. Children yawn and writhe. Syshe—the snottiest of the children (everyone agrees)—throws herself back in her chair with Pixérécourtian drama. Time-withered extracts from *National Geographic* and dubiously colored inkjet printouts—the Amazon as seen from the Içana, Schwarzwald in Baden-Württemberg, Arashiyama in Japan—freckle the wall between windows overlooking the concrete play court. The outside wall has likewise been painted with a mural of trees, and Ori feels, with the pang of watching a clown totter atop a tightrope, what it is to be both amused and distressed. Later, when the fidgeting students are asked to draw their hands, Ori instead draws a tree, with her fingers for the branches. By now, the teacher has moved on to multiplication tables, but Ori is not listening. She is transfixed by a faded image, harvested from a coffee table book, of the towering sequoias of Redwood National Park.

Ori is in love.

That night, having been tucked in, she dreams of birthday parties for trees, of gently pulling back her skin to find six concentric rings. She wiggles her toes, metatarsals wriggling like roots.

The following afternoon, she tells her mother that she is going to her piano lesson. She tells her piano teacher that she is going home.

It is the perfect crime.

She locates the Shop of Natural Wonders at Avery and 6th, right where the internet said it would be. In the front window, a sprawling watercolor display connotes the phyla and genera of various trees in illegible cursive. Ori studies it for a moment, uncannily reminded of diagrams of algorithms she's seen. She is too young to register the "stem" pun but is nonetheless eagerly impressed by this confluence of dendrology and abstract mathematics.

Inside is a wonderland of buckets and boxes, devotedly lit and brimming with impossible greens. Amid a riot of ponytail palms and fiddle-leaf figs, beneath a sign that reads WELCOME TO THE POST-ANTHROPOCENE, a shopkeeper looks up from their ancient-looking desk.

"May I help you?" they say, and Ori feels like the clown atop the tightrope.

She clears her throat.

"I am dreaming of a tree," she says, doing her best to remember how adults speak. Then, consulting her little phone, perfectly sized for her hand, "A *Sequoia sempervirens*."

The shopkeeper smiles. "A redwood."

"Yes."

The shopkeeper stands and, gauging Ori to be serious, disappears into an adjacent room. A moment later, they reemerge from the inner sanctum with a special box: part plastic, part earth.

"It's twenty seeds," they say. "Plant them all. At best, one will grow."

Ori takes the box. Such a serious, delicate thing. From the innermost compartment of her bumblebee backpack, she produces the small fortune that she has been saving for ice cream.

The deal is done.

She buries the seeds in the earth, at the center of the park, then spits on them for good luck.

Syshe, en route home from school, crinkles her button nose at the sight of Ori's hands, etched with dirt. "What are you doing?" she sneers.

Ori is unfazed. "Planting the tallest tree in the world."

Syshe sagely announces, "You'll be dead when it gets that tall."

But Ori looks up toward her home, a sliver of mirror, imagining leaves in the reflection. Her mouth twitches with the slight, shimmering half smile of one who knows better.

She will not be dead. She'll be immortal.

All the Places You Will Never Be Again

A CAMERA IS A little room, she's saying, a chamber, in Latin, you know, and then it's in her hands, thick with ink, bleeding onto the glossy square like an omen. She's towering over you on the mattress, shaking the Polaroid like you've seen people do in movies, her legs quivering for balance beneath a pair of popcorn-yellow underwear. She is steel and sweat, jacket but no blouse, all teeth. A man-made wonder.

When she touches you it's like a blister, the sensation dialed up too high to be real, and this is when you know, like when the earth shakes in Iowa or the moon rises twice, that you are not awake.

This is a frequent one, as is the one where you meet at that blush-brick, corn-scented all-girls school in the heart of true nowhere, a blur of plaid and touched knees and pencil lead speared, initial after initial, into the wood of your desk. You count this among all the places you will never be again. There and here.

The photograph's of you, of course, invincibly coy, an almost-smile frozen in time. She's blithering about *La tache aveugle*, some French film you've never seen, where a figure materializes, nothing to something. Invisible to visible. Like you, she's saying, the Polaroid box slung across her bare chest. She presents the photo for inspection and she's right: that pinned-down smile of yours blossoms from sheer absence to a ghost, to something that looks exactly like you.

There are boxes of these things: little squares of you in a sundress, you at the grocery, you on a boat. Whose boat, you can't recall.

You've never understood why she took so many. Could she have been afraid, even then, of forgetting? Of missed pills and buried parents, years like rooms where the lights turn on and off without rationale, scattered faces and addresses, events softening and sliding together like dirt in rain?

She bites your ear at the top, the part called the helix, she's saying, the unruly dark blur of her hair in your mouth and your eyes, and there's another click and whir of the machine, a new square, another you.

When you wake up, she'll be her again and you'll be you. She'll be five times her age, the age she is now, clove smoke and chenin blanc, a knee on either side of you. You'll be immortal, a slew of you in the box.

She's asked for it to be brought here, to the hospital. This box of photographs. This box of yous. She's shown you a photograph with which she's especially thrilled, you smoking a cigarette, fresh out of the shower, fingers splayed as though to ward off the lens, but even in this moment, you're elsewhere. It's not real, you're saying, it's the false you, the you of the photographs, the impeccable you, the you of never again and bliss-stricken now. The you who is always awake.

The room is itself a little chamber, a camera (in Latin, you know), an angular box of single incidents. Announcings, acceptings, hand-squeezings, tracheal insertions, shots, cures, last rites, last words, deaths. Births, maybe. This isn't that part of the hospital. Everything is eggshell plastic and recycled sheets, the knit blue blankets pale and rippled, like the ones you pretended were the ocean as a child. Her fingers are curled around the box in her lap, like roots around a stone jutting up from the earth, and this is how she sleeps.

You sleep, too, curled in the waxy pink shell of a chair beside her, although sleep is a strong word.

There are things you'll miss, she's saying. That's la tache aveugle.

But what if you catch them in time? you say. And there's nothing you can do?

She is unfazed. She's talking about silver halide grains, interlayers, and image dyes. She has always insisted on the *science*, science above all, the way the pieces collapse on themselves, layer on layer, catalyzed by time. You remarked once, in a world other than this one, the real world, on the irony that science couldn't save her. Big deal, she had said. Science has better things to do.

She bites the pieces of you as though she could keep them, your neck and nose, your hair and little finger. She is magic and misery, a flicker of herself. The nimble, hazy goddess you imagine her to be, like a manuscript on which coffee has been spilled.

You look up and it's like seeing her through water. She wavers as though being shaken.

She's shown you the pyramids, dragged you to the exhibit of the mummified gazelle—the pharaoh's pet, can you imagine? she's saying —and you can. You can imagine.

She'll want to be buried with these photographs. At first you'll hate the thought of it, that much of you beneath the earth. But you'll come around, knowing that when she dies, so much of you will be down there anyway.

When she wakes, she'll ask for her favorite thing, which is to see the thin negative layers of plastic laid on top of each other, cell after cell, demonstrating the steady, greedy march of her condition. She never remembers which disease it is, what she has. Good for her.

She'll turn to you, not remembering that she's said this before, and say, Isn't it something?

It is, you say, it is something. Then she's back into the box of photographs and you hate how many are of you, they're all of you—Why didn't you take more pictures of her? You're the one who will need them.

Still, she is transfixed by the thick greens and blues, the interlaced fingers and sheets, the summers of bangs and corduroy, the local politics, the attempts to kill a lobster you had not realized would be sold to you alive.

You have seen the pharaoh, and you are the gazelle.

Insertion

SHE THINKS OF ALL the things that have been inside her—the fingers and tongues, of course, but beyond that, the Matchbox car she swallowed on a dare; the small but still too-large-to-be-swallowed umeboshi plum; the injected titanium filament in her right breast when they were quite confident (but not confident enough not to inject the filament) that she did not have cancer; the ink of the tattoo over her left breast (consistently cancer-free); the sewing needle home-piercing above her left eye, sterilized in Bacardi 151 (now discontinued) and delivered, implausibly, stone-sober, still elegantly scarred; the later follow-up piercing, inflicted for seventy Australian dollars in a proper, bliss-white *2001: A Space Odyssey*–redolent parlor, soon thereafter irrevocably dislodged when she traipsed into a clothesline at night;

teeth-whitening strips; innumerable toothbrushes; over six thousand tampons; 9,234ish multivitamins; 240ish spiders (if statistical science is to be believed); the neck of the wine bottle that chipped her tooth, hastily but effectively filed down at a tearfully negotiated discount in the wee hours before reporting to the office; the necks of other bottles of other things, consumed under less celebratory conditions; Q-tips; under-the-tongue thermometers; ear thermometers; once, a meat thermometer; a neti pot, swiftly rejected; toothpicks; anal beads; lollipops from the doctor's office; lollipops from the bank drive-thru; upward of fifty-seven thousand pounds of food; 43.5 gallons of alcohol; needles; the lip of a pipe, on numerous occasions for marijuana and once for heroin (the latter infinitely regretted); Fun Dip sticks, sparingly dipped; vaccinations; hoop earrings; stud earrings; a minuscule vibrator won in a Halloween stage competition at a now-defunct Hollywood club, likely at least in part defunct because they were handing out free vibrators; silverware; plasticware; slivers from fences; specula; once, irreversibly, a curette; tongue depressors; a globule of gluey jade-green wax, the good stuff, twirled and ripped from her nostrils on the occasion of her first and final nose wax; inadvertently swallowed gum; the blade of a knife; the butt of a knife; the barrel of a fake gun; the barrel of a real gun, just to see; the lips of balloons; a glittering array of dental instruments; the tracheal tube, just that once; tweezers; braces; caps of pens; guitar picks; wire-thin tendrils of floss, again and again and again—all nothing, as skin is nothing, as organs are exchangeable, insofar as sacred though the body may purportedly be, it is still, now as ever, dust-to-dust, plastic and steel, a quilt of invasion.

Cain vs. Cain

OF COURSE HE REMEMBERS the goddamn sandwich board. "Today's soup: the tears of our enemies." Jay's subsequent promotion at the Rabbit Hole (presumably on account of being so goddamn clever), was immediately followed by Jasper's now-infamous Yelp review, in which a web-savvy sixty-five-year-old woman had graphically described how the new manager had sexually assaulted her service dog (which was also pretty goddamn clever). Both boys had (of course) been fired. Both had (of course) told the other he quit.

Now, in the fragile Chinese paper lantern glow of their boyhood tent, Jasper and Jay share the contents of their father's dented flask. "People like us," says Jasper, "we need wars."

"Do we?" says Jay, but of course he agrees. Outside the tent, the blistery red licks of the fire jot skyward in fits and starts.

"Don't come crying to me if this turns into some 'Telltale Heart' shit for you," says Jasper.

"I won't," says Jay.

The trip had been Jay's idea, a kind of campy ode to the past twenty years, which had been a kind of campy ode to the first twenty chapters of *Fight Club*. The last time either could remember having functioned amicably is when they'd vowed to date the Olsen twins together in the fourth grade. The years since had been a cavalcade of escalating transgressions, each more Andronican than the last.

E.g., on account of Jasper (who claims to be a vegetarian), Jay no longer has pets larger or more sentimental than a goldfish.

E.g., on account of Jay (who claims to be straight as a proverbial arrow), Jasper no longer mentions when he's engaged.

"This is reminding me of something," says Jasper.

"Genesis?" says Jay.

"No, the summer after kindergarten," says Jasper.

Beneath a swath of violet, the indifferent fire laps at the collapse of a log. Or a femur. Jay pours another shock of liquid into the speckled aluminum mugs.

"What is this shit?" says Jasper.

"Amontillado," says Jay.

"Cute," says Jasper.

The click of the toast becomes a kind of mirror, each hunting down the slight genetic deviations, the shape of the brows, any rogue curvature of the hairline. A rubbery, earthy stench of flannel and DEET and Neanderthal impartiality and drugstore cologne winds its way beneath the rift of the tent flap.

"Why did you hate him?" says Jay.

"Because he loved you more," says Jasper. "What about you?"

"Because he loved us the same," says Jay.

Tomorrow, they will almost certainly relapse. Even now, behind the near-orgasmic flicker of unity, each is silently coiling an exquisite plot to pin this on the other with the precision of a boutonniere. Each will be up before dawn, jockeying for who calls the National Park Service to file the report, scuffing each other's boots with the ashes.

Tonight, they'll talk late into the night, each adoring the other as the best lesser version of himself, roasting marshmallows over the embers.

The Body Electric

SHE SINGS THE body electric. That's her joke.

It began as an act of charity— part political act, part publicity stunt—but by the end of 1895, it had become something else entirely. Something profoundly less hers and yet solely hers. (Everyone else was dead, after all.)

In a grandly poetic slaughter of two birds with one stone, her agent had prescribed a gesture of selflessness that would concurrently remind the greater New York Metropolitan audience of her gift. The papers lapped it up like the glamorous, grotesque gimmick it was, and struggled for weeks to transform her name into some variation on "Angel of Death." In the end, they settled lazily on "the Singer of Sing Sing."

Now, with the casually majestic gait of a high priestess, Eleanor

Echols glides through the prison halls, her delicate heels ratting a *tack-tack-tack* behind the heavier, more sinister *tock-tock-tock* of the warden's boots. At first, the warden is bleakly inhospitable, skeptical. Later, he will become an avid admirer of her work, and still later he will come to fear her.

She is warned, many times, by everyone, of the delicacy of the proceedings. Women faint, she is told. They weep. They wake in the night for the rest of their lives, unable to unsee what they've witnessed in this little room at the end of so many cells, bone-white and stark as the sacrum at the end of a spinal cord. She takes in each bloated masculine warning with polite, thin-lipped restraint. Eleanor has a weapon against all such adverse reactions:

She feels nothing.

This quality—this unfashionable, superhuman absence of emotion—makes her the perfect accessory to the present scene: the execution of a prisoner.

The subject of today's proceedings, a glorified skeleton in sagging cotton, is led in and seated in the chair at center. He is asked to extend his arms, to sit upright, to press his head back. He is cooperative and dead-eyed. He regards his assigned entourage—a chaplain, a set of doctors, the warden, the technician, a handful of bystanders in wool suits—with a grimace that is at once transcendent and lush with hate.

There is an obvious novelty to the presence of a woman, so the inmate nods in Eleanor's direction. "Who's she?"

"She's here to sing thee to thy rest, sweet prince," the technician replies with equal parts conviviality and disdain. "She's from the New York Metropolitan Opera. What do you think of that?"

The prisoner scoffs and studies her, cocks a brow. "Do you know 'Carry Me Back to Old Virginny'?"

"I do not," Eleanor replies flatly.

The inmate laughs. "Ah, I'm fucking joking," he says. "Sing whatever you're going to sing."

"Do not swear in the presence of a lady," says the warden.

"Or indeed at all," says the chaplain.

Eleanor smiles a narrow, unfeeling smile. "Let him swear," she says. "It's his fucking execution."

Eleanor places her small handbag on the floor, since there is no other furniture in the room. The chaplain clutches his leather-bound brick of a Bible and steps back, watching attentively, while the guards and witnesses position themselves in a ring, arms crossed, expectant and amused.

Eleanor stands before the prisoner, straightens her dress.

She opens her mouth and sings:

> Non c'è vita
> Se non nella memoria
> Non c'è amore
> Se non nell'elegia

She had assiduously shopped the collections in the opera's library, rifling through volumes surging with Gounod, Bellini, Caldara, Puccini. At long last, she had arrived at her present aria with the gratified rush of a magician having mastered a sleight-of-hand act. Most opera is about death, as she is fond of saying, but this one seemed especially unimpressed with the state of being alive.

> There is no life
> But in memory
> There is no love
> But in elegy

The warden and his men watch with spellbound rigor, touched to the quick.

The chaplain watches from the edge of the room with a ripple of envy, knowing that his last rites will have no such effect.

Eleanor glissandos upward to a spectacular climax, a trill that begins in her legs and ends somewhere beyond the top of her head, in the ether. She marvels at the acoustics of this little room, the electric chair at center its gravitational core.

She finishes her song, and all is silent. At last, the warden nods toward one of his men. "Charlie here'll take you back."

"I'll stay," she says.

What follows is a cavalcade of warnings she's already heard, a blow-by-blow of the emotional ramifications of the event, a condescending treatise on death, too dire and disturbing for the fragile feminine psyche.

"I'll stay," she says again.

The warden hesitates, then squints his good eye and nods curtly toward the technician. The technician shrugs as if to say, "Your funeral," but Eleanor stays focused on the prisoner. She wonders, fleetingly, if he'd prefer to be hanged.

Eleanor watches as a leather strap is placed over the eyes, another over the mouth. A stiff, sturdy band is wound around the chest, another across the hips. One for each leg. She watches as the shallow metal salad bowl affixed to a spiral of wire is placed over his head, like a crude preparation for a schoolboy's haircut.

"Sing," he says suddenly.

The technician stops his adjustments, had clearly suspended thinking of the limbs beneath his grip as belonging to a human being.

"Sing," the inmate repeats, his chin tilted toward Eleanor beneath the dual straps shielding his eyes and mouth. "And don't stop till I'm dead."

Two months later, it's a woman.

The usual attendees hang near the outskirts of the room, watching like zoo-goers for some semblance of feminine compassion or connection, camaraderie. But the prisoner is here because she's drowned her children, and Eleanor is here for the press. She watches with curiosity as the prisoner's stockings are rolled down, the band wound around her waist like she's a 110-pound doll. The men stand back, decades of holding doors and assisting descents from carriages coiled in their limbs. They regard the prisoner like she's an animal, as they must if they're to pull the lever.

No one lectures Eleanor about psychology today.

She sings a Verdi, a bit too jaunty for the occasion, but lovely nonetheless.

She stays (she always stays) to watch the body crackle and jolt, the tautening of the veins beneath the paper-thin flesh of the throat, the scent of mis-cooked meat in the air. She presses her palms backward against the slick gray-white wall behind her, fingers splayed. She feels herself a ghost, leaking into concrete and oak, at once her and not her, some other thing.

Sometimes, after, she'll stand in Longacre Square, looking up, envisioning everything the place might one day be, electric and thrumming. She still performs at the New York Metropolitan, but finds herself progressively more revulsed with the audience. They are distracted, pallid, devoid of urgency. She stands on stage, picking out the elderly whose pearls or tie pins stretch against their necks and torsos. She pictures these items as leather bands, squeezing their skin into sections, jarring them into a final, bewildering moment of being alive. She imagines them dying, betrayed by their own lungs, their own hearts, eyes bulging with surprise, ruining everyone else's night.

Eventually, the papers grow bored with Eleanor's outings. Public attention reverts to the most original and grisliest of the crimes themselves: the beheadings, the burnings, the dismemberments, the partial torsos drifting down the Hudson atop swollen rafts of intestines and sinew. Eleanor reads of each new exploit, insensate as ever, but her apathy has begun to lap at the edges of something grimmer, more exhilarating.

With each new execution, Eleanor makes the trek north along the river as though drawn by an invisible thread. Today she brings with her a new, improvised aria: Walt Whitman set to the tune of an ancient

Cavalli. She watches as the technician straps down the inmate's limbs with fluid precision.

Eleanor straightens her dress, and begins to sing:

> The thin red jellies within you or within me,
> the bones and the marrow in the bones,
> The exquisite realization of health;
> O I say these are not the parts and poems of the body only,
> but of the soul,
> O I say now these are the soul!

The music swells within her, blistering and pulsing like a current. The guards, the witnesses, the chaplain, the technician, the warden look on in a state of mesmerized stillness.

Then the lever is switched, and the spell is broken.

There are three rooms for condemned female inmates at the prison. Tonight, Eleanor, the Singer of Sing Sing, occupies the third.

They had found the body (or most of it, at least) in her dressing room at the opera house. Rumors had immediately begun to circulate of some wild, rampant envy surging through her veins like a viral infection. A lover's quarrel, neurotic passion, familial betrayal. But it was none of these things, of course. Only a stranger who had nodded off during the overture, then awoken during the second act and checked his pocket watch within Eleanor's view.

Eleanor's heels rap a familiar rhythm along the concrete of the last mile, a treble at odds with the bass of the warden's boots. She sits in the chair without being asked, in this room where she has been a hundred times. The technician adjusts her bands with discomfited reverence, a lurking mélange of respect and fear.

Eleanor does not dread the sensation of the electrical current. She knows that the body will be, in this moment, more alive than it has ever been.

The warden reads the final decision. The chaplain says his benediction. The witnesses watch, and wait.

The technician pulls the lever.

Eleanor feels everything at once.

And she begins to sing.

The Lady Will Pay for Everything

ކޮ ދޮސަރުޤް ރުޢިރަޒ އާރުޤޭކަޢަ ޤޭސި ޤަޟަޢާޢެސެ

THE FISH COME FROM nowhere. They are at once, suddenly, everywhere.

Ian is the first to notice. He traces the glass, his knobby finger squeaking erratically against the pristine blue sheen of the window. The window is, of course, also the wall, also the ceiling, very nearly the floor, arching in an extravagant curve over the scope of the living area. The place is a luxurious little glass balloon, a bubble-shaped dollhouse, tastefully ascetic amid a riot of coral and blindingly blue Indian Ocean. The fish is the color of wine, a honeycomb of scales etched in popsicle-green, lips bright orange, eyes candy-red.

"What do we do?" Ian says.

"We only kill spiders indoors," Marie says sagely, and goes back to her paper. "Leave him alone."

"How do you know it's a him?" says Ian.

But Marie is no longer listening. She is entrenched in the *Times*, a civilized treat squirreled away from home, a bastion of what people are saying nine thousand miles away and fifty-nine feet above. In any case, she isn't a monster. Isn't it maternal enough to have brought her children here, to have given them the experience of a lifetime?

Leslie traipses in with her suitcase. It and she are both daintily small. She plops her luggage onto the carpet and looks around, gracefully nonplussed. "Should we be down here?" she says, but the way she says it sounds like something else, something worse.

Marie loves her daughter, more than life itself (more than Ian), but there is a queasy sort of reverence, a fear and awe of the misunderstood, in her devotion. Leslie had come out perfectly—a short but draining labor for which Marie had been blissfully stoned—but with her skull slightly raised in the back (had Marie pushed hard enough? fast enough?) beneath an enviable swirl of wispy baby-blond hair. This minor malformation, together with a nearly translucent complexion and pistachio-green eyes, gave her a slightly alien aesthetic. A few days after Leslie was born, Marie had begun to brutally, pragmatically scour a gamut of fashion magazines. She subscribed to everything, riffled through the pages with a ferocious, jungle-cat vengeance. She was looking for models who looked like her baby—lengthy and lithe, nearly diaphanous—ensuring safety for another season. So far, so good.

Ian presses his nose against the glass. The fish does the same.

"Look, Mama!" says Ian, and Marie pretends to look. She watches instead as Leslie takes a full step backward and sits at the center of the room, peaceably bored.

"Can we go swimming?" says Ian.

"No," says Marie. There is a small elevator at the remote end of the suite, which rises to a slatted dock, where a narrow ladder dangles into the ocean. But that's the trouble with a transparent underwater hotel. One can see the sharks, rays, hawkfish, barracuda.

One knows too much.

. . .

Christian had learned of the جِسْر underwater resort from someone
else at the firm. Christian's colleague said it had "changed his life,"
though Marie couldn't fathom what was so special about his life to
begin with. Ultimately, Christian had persuaded her with an orches-
trated slideshow of Google images and the promise of exclusivity, an
experience she could lord over her friends and weaponize against her
social media rivals.

Marie had hated it instantly. It was like being relegated to the basement during a family reunion—private, yes, but so much obviously
worse than upstairs. And it was small, oddly shaped in the style of a
row house or submarine, bathed in a distortion-prone, perpetually
marbled blue light. What would her friends say? All her pictures would
look the same.

"Listen, I'll pay for everything," Christian had said. He had often
said this, since the earliest phases of their courtship, sparking in Marie
something between obligatory indignation and massive relief. Marie
had laughed. As though money were the problem, her and the children
footing their portion of the bill. She was apoplectically bitter, but there
was, as always, an overwhelming sense of ease, being married to this
wonderfully rich dumb fuck.

"It'll be the experience of a lifetime," Christian had said. Marie had
cheerfully repeated this expression to their children, and here they were.

In her youth, Marie had felt a strange, precarious disquiet when visiting aquariums. Unreasonable, she knew, but she dreaded the giant ves-
tibules of glass, electric with jellyfish or swarming with African cichlids,
certain the glass would break and the foreign world would come spilling
onto her shoes, subsequently drowning the entire field trip. Here, she
realizes, in this meticulously designed bunker of glass and stone, they
are the aquarium.

The hotel's remoteness is the crux of its charm—that's what Christian
keeps saying—but the methods of travel required to get here had seemed
endless, each more exhausting and antiquarian than the last. There was

the cab to JFK, then the shuttle, then the plane to Hong Kong, then the smaller, worse plane to Sri Lanka, then the boat. God, the *boat*. They had weaved through little islands with names like Gemanafushi and Rathafandhoo, impossible little scraps of earth atop an undulating sheet of crystalline blue. Christian had observed all this with the doe-eyed incredulity of a student on his first school outing. Marie had never hated him more.

Ian places his nose against the glass and taps, taps, taps. On the opposite side of the window, his iridescent, ichthyoid acquaintance does the same. Then the latter turns, slick and shimmering, and returns to its school.

The morning passes without incident. Leslie stumbles back and forth across the living area, clumsily mirroring the path of stingrays and undersized sharks overhead. Christian lies on the carpet alongside Ian, making a big show of pointing out various creatures—scorpionfishes, cow sharks, tripletails, emperors, goatfishes—although Marie suspects he's making it all up. Ian writhes in laughter, imagining fish as the animals they're named for. Leslie watches as Marie fetches a pashmina from the master bedroom, then hops up from the carpet and follows her mother to the elevator.

The surface-level patio had been a selling point in Christian's pitch. Now, here, Marie is, at best, underwhelmed. The patio is a stripe of wood in the middle of true nowhere, saved from its identity as a raft only by concrete pylons and an exorbitant price tag.

"Where will we go for Christmas?" says Leslie.

"Wherever you want," says Marie, although this is patently untrue.

Marie and Leslie dangle their legs in the water, a flirt with danger. They have seen the goatfishes.

The chef arrives, a spry, unpretentious local named Aiham whose credentials from Le Cordon Bleu seem highly suspect. The children flock to him, enchanted by his sun-flecked complexion and satchel of food, which holds the combined mystique of a magician's kit and medic's bag. "Aiham!" Christian exclaims, his mispronunciation drenched with confidence. "What have you brought us?"

"Papaya, kohlrabi, and . . ." Aiham lifts a final prize from his bag with a sorcerer's flourish: "وَمُوَرَسُ."

The last of these items, a flat, shimmering tuna, dangles from his fist, rivulets of dirt and salt in the gills. Leslie steps forward to touch it, but Marie swats her hand away. "It's raw," she says. "You have no idea where it's been." Later, the children will marvel that they can eat something they aren't allowed to touch.

Aiham likes to tell stories as he cooks, and tonight his pleasure is a Maldivian folk tale about birds. "You might not like it," he says. But the children are insistent, and in the end he cedes to their whims above the languidly amused, politely impatient expressions of their parents.

"There is an island," Aiham begins, "which is not perfect, for nothing ever was, but that was once the closest thing to paradise you could imagine. It was a sanctuary for a flock of seabirds, chosen especially by the god of the sea. One night, a land bird arrived at the island, weary from travel. He begged the birds of the island to let him stay, just for one night. The leader of the island—a wise old seabird—warned his companions that if they let the visitor stay, the island (or at least their way of life on the island) would be destroyed forever. The leader spoke with great passion, but his power was limited (as you may know, birds are democratic), and the seabirds decided to let the visitor stay. In the morning, the land bird awoke from his roost on the beach, thanked his hosts, and flew away. Nothing bad had happened. The seabirds laughed at the old leader, and congratulated themselves on their generosity. But the following day, a strange tree began to grow on the beach. The land bird's droppings had contained a seed from another island, and soon enough, the seed sprouted and blossomed into a coconut tree. Soon there were more and more trees, until the beach was thick with them. New birds, new animals, and finally human travelers arrived, eager to harvest the fruit of the trees. The humans shot the seabirds and ate them, and wore their feathers as jewelry."

Leslie and Ian listen in rapt silence as Aiham speaks. When he finishes, Christian clears his throat. "Does the hotel know you tell stories like that?"

Aiham laughs. "There are no other guests here in the off-season. *You* are the hotel," he says.

That night, Leslie cannot sleep. She retrieves a box of colored pencils from a secret compartment of her suitcase, along with a sheaf of plain white computer paper, and sets to work.

She draws the fish as they are, magnificent and terrifying. She draws the prickly little buttons of coral and macaroni tendrils of anemone.

She considers the floor of the ocean, beneath the carpeted floor beneath her feet, and draws this little patch of earth and sea—wildly sumptuous, insatiably violent—as it might have been, as it would have been, had their present accommodations never been built.

Christian gets up in the dark, slips on the plush pair of بحر branded slippers beside the bed. He crosses through the eerily lit master bath, a wonderland of sea glass and stone, past the elevator and dining area, into the living room. He pauses at the closed door of the children's room on the opposite side, fingertips resting on the brushed metal handle. He would swear he hears little scratches—Leslie's pencil set or a scraping of fingertips against glass—coming from inside. He leaves the door and helps himself to an ambiguously expensive, unrecognized bottle from the blue crystal bar. Glass on glass on glass. He turns back toward the window, which is also the wall, also the ceiling, very nearly the floor. He leans his forehead against the surface, curious to see what all the fuss is about.

But no fish come, and Christian goes back to bed.

Leslie and Ian have begun to walk differently, slackening their limbs and swiveling as though moving through water. Marie watches them with lax amusement, envious of their capacity to make the most of such a ridiculous family vacation.

She imagines them now as a quartet of underwater sentries, ancient statues in a range of poses: fighting an underwater war, building an underwater barracks, planting an underwater garden. She imagines tourists coming to visit them, descending the narrow glass block of the elevator, taking photos with their phones sheathed in waterproof cases.

The fish comes back, this time with friends. The entire school—dozens, then hundreds of fish—race in a silvery kaleidoscope of laps around the hotel. Ian is thrilled, dashes from the living area to the bedroom through the bathroom and kitchenette, attempting to match their speed with the alacrity of a puppy chasing a car.

At long last, he returns to the living area, exhausted. He collapses on the floor, near Marie's graceful perch on one of the living room chairs. Leslie continues to draw, her colored pencils weaving in merciless strings of sherbet orange and cerulean blue, watermelon pink and electric lime. Each fish appears to be not merely a fish, but all fish at once.

Marie, who voraciously collects and half-heartedly pretends to understand art, glances at the raft of white computer paper surrounding Leslie. She makes a mental note to keep an eye on this habit, to nurture it if needed, to bring Leslie to the next Gagosian opening and see how she responds.

A fish hovers idly just beyond the glass, then smacks its fluorescent pink maw into the window. It does this again, again and again and again. More fish arrive, a wriggling swarm of speckled fins and glimmering scales. The fish's snout blossoms into a delicate spray of blood, whiskers that sprout and slither outward in every direction.

The windows love the blood, seem to be hungry for it. Droplets of red freckle and smear like rain on a windshield. Christian is already on the phone, calling hotel management. Ian has stopped running. Leslie has dotted her slew of drawing paper with pimples of crimson, poison apple, brick red. Marie is reading about the Dow and its subservience to foreign markets.

It is a special kind of glass, and when it breaks, it cracks in a clean, straight fissure, like two halves of a plastic Easter egg. Leslie is the first to understand what's happening. She takes her brother's hand and stares across the living area. The light above them, slick with blood, wavers with an ethereal sheen.

The children stare at their parents, as though having rehearsed this, and the ocean falls like a curtain between them.

Marie is nearest the elevator and stumbles toward it, fists of ocean curling about her ankles. A crack of glass erupts behind her and a swirl of water slams against the backs of her knees. She reaches the lift bay and slaps the button. She looks up, into the very real tunnel and toward the light. The lift drops down, inexorably slowly, designed to resist sudden changes in pressure and to maximize the view.

When the water reaches her waist, she hears herself scream, a nightmare scream of trivial volume. And then, as though casually visiting a familiar place, the fish are in her hair and mouth, squirming between her legs and swirling around her neck. Christian is elsewhere, dead already, arms spread wide as though to say: one day this will all be yours.

Silence prevails, dense with a percussion of glass and heaviness of ocean. Amid the water, vast and violet with blood, the silk sheets sway like kelp; artwork puckers and disintegrates; the top-shelf whiskey is irretrievably watered down. Already the vases have become nests; pillows blossom with squirrelfish and sprats. Fish are everywhere, an eye on each side, seeing everything.

Eruptions of light freckle Marie's vision. With her second-to-last thought, she mourns herself, then, fearful of some cosmic reprisal for her ego, thinks of the children. She imagines the fish taking pity on them, like wolves in fairytales, raising them as their own.

She feels herself becoming a nest.

She imagines Leslie breathing underwater, and hopes she's not too old to learn.

Eating the Leaves

SHE STARTS TRAINING for everything at once: motherhood, the apocalypse, a 5K. The Pulitzer-winning earthquake that promises to obliterate the Pacific Northwest. A high-altitude decathlon. North Korea.

She stops drinking (but still drinks some, because obviously, the world is terrible and who can bear it?), stockpiles prenatals, buys new shoes. Functional shoes.

She reads a book about real/whole/just-totally-no-holds-barred-fucking-totally-real food and the pleasures of a radiant pregnancy. She skips presumptuous chapters contingent upon the handy availability of tropical organic produce.

She goes to the woods and looks around, hard. She is underwhelmed by the prowess of the survival guide illustrator. She intently wants to recognize the edible leaves—to discern poison from nutrition—but they all look the same, green on green on green.

Days pass. Weeks. She gets better books, listens to podcasts, writes her senator. She runs, everywhere, but always, ultimately, to nowhere, sleeps the thick black sleep of the irretrievably exhausted. She buys walkie-talkies, wonders to whom she should give the second device.

She rejects excess, donates wildly.

She wades through old photographs, despising them—their flat immortality, their shallow, bulletproof intimacy.

She returns to the woods—marginally older, the same—pockets packed with color print-outs of leaves.

She studies the earth, glides her thumbs over the flimsy fawn-soft green. Panic rises in her like a fist, a tight and bloody, aching thing.

She studies the photos. But every leaf looks like a leaf, especially the ones that will kill you.

Even so, now, while the hospitals still run on power and the mountain is standing and there's no propitious alien lifeform blossoming in her gut, she must learn.

So she plucks a leaf—a leaf that looks as much like the artist's rendering as any leaf—and she begins to eat.

Mnemophobe

ANIKA HATES ISÉLA the way she hates people who win cars from radio stations. More than four-pound sinecure service dogs who shiver and piss on airplanes, more than interrupting others to insist on the correct pronunciation of Ibiza, more than the wage gap, Anika hates Iséla. This hate, sulking and seething, licks at the curves of her brain, distracts her during work, disrupts her sleep.

Anika vividly recalls—more colorfully but less accurately each time—the horrendous plaid of the basement couch, designed as though for the express purpose of deterring sex; the decidedly local haircut of Iséla at age sixteen; her baseline resemblance to Penélope Cruz in a halo of Miller Lite; the TV on, ignored; Iséla's fingernails, self-painted, discount blue; a half-consumed bag of chips, ripped open at a devil-may-care angle; the sliver of sky through garden-view windows blushing into a kind of warning, early-a.m. pink; nail polishes fumblingly compared, a lattice of fingertips; lip balms, likewise poised for a joking-then-serious comparison; *Leave It to Beaver* drifting, unnoticed, into the local news.

Because this is a dream, and therefore nonsense, Anika is now famous, and Conan O'Brien is asking, via inexplicable dream logic, "Who was your first kiss?"

The audience hoots, desperate to know. Needing this.

"Iséla," she says, viciously coy. The audience hoots louder, an exploded sixth grade locker room.

"And . . . ?" Conan presses.

Anika examines her nails, a chic lemon-meringue yellow, with careless, offhand finesse. "It was . . . fine." An exquisite, flawless snub. Somewhere, Iséla kills herself.

She only lives in that little town—Redfield, but really South Dakota, all of it—for one year. But it's a formative year. The things people say are all in the neutral, nowhere dialect of Bob Barker and Tom Brokaw, a trustworthy nothingness. She senses its power, this nowhere-voice, and learns how to do it. She moves away and is fine, better than fine. Still, her revenge fantasy languishes just beneath the skin, underscored by the grating laughter of Andy Richter, couched in the imagined, incorrectly remembered upholstery of the overstuffed Conan O'Brien chairs.

In subsequent years, Anika sits hunched in the dull blue glow of her computer screen, Avi (textbook, unimpeachably husbandlike) faintly snoring in the darkness behind her. Through the vapid dark magic of the internet, she clocks the recurrence of Iséla's acne with wincing pleasure. The grapes, as it turns out, are in fact sour.

Of course, as any oenophile will tell you, sour grapes—on occasion —become wine.

Shortly thereafter, on the advice of no one, Anika wends her way through her class reunion, gripping a cup of Riesling like an enemy throat. She shouldn't have come—Avi warned her not to, smelling on this excursion the unburied body of a former self. Yet here she is, weaving through a sea of thin-lipped housewives and shriveling jawlines— hating them all, hating everything to the nth—toward her magnet, her nemesis . . . Iséla.

Iséla is now, infuriatingly and exhilaratingly, sans acne. "Your face," says Anika.

Iséla smiles, a maddeningly perfect smile. "No, yours."

They are at once a tangle of fingers—fingers Anika has often fantasized of snapping in half, denailing, tormenting with an obscure iteration of mislearned acupressure-as-torture, now interlaced with hers.

Tonight will be an ecstatic blur of possibility, not yet misremembered. They will kiss. Anika will cry; Iséla will not object. She will feel what it is to hold a world, fragile and aching, in one's palm.

To open one's fist and find it gone.

Orphan Type

HELEN—FRESHLY ORPHANED and appreciably unmoored—traverses the hall as though in a dream. Beneath the jittering glow of a lantern, the pocky gray slab of a floor comes into view. It is, upon closer inspection, dappled with tiny footprints etched in black ink.

Unconscionably drawn forward, Helen continues down the hall, her young face shaded with early-onset melancholy. A faint, metronomic *drip . . . drip . . . drip . . .* escalates in volume as she rounds a corner. Ink drips into a small puddle at her feet. She raises the lantern.

Above, framed by jagged shadows, are a slew of child-sized, skinned bodies, dangling from the ceiling like slabs of meat.

Helen jolts awake.

There are no bodies—none dead, at least—only a room full of

sleeping children. Each lies on a wire cot, tangled or draped with the same striped sheet issued upon arrival. Helen's, issued just that afternoon, is damp with sweat. Barely visible through the dusty, moon-dappled darkness, the children's tiny frames undulate as they breathe. Even in sleep, they have the appearance of little soldiers, weary and nondescript. Helen thinks of the photographs she's seen of the Great War, men propped on elbows, blank-eyed and resolute. Gray on gray. Indeed, aside from the average size of its guests—children here range in age from five to fifteen—the room would be virtually indistinguishable from an army barracks.

This is the orphan workforce of the *New Haven Herald*.

On the cot beside Helen, Ruthie—or *Ruth*, rather, as she's insisted on being called since turning nine—lies trembling, asleep but restless. Beneath a set of dark bangs, Ruthie's countenance is stoic, brow furrowed, glossy with tears. Helen traces her cheek, softly enough not to wake her, then gently peels back each finger from Ruthie's tightly curled fist. Clamped inside, a locket barely glints in the dark. Helen carefully pries it from her grasp, then runs the pad of her thumb over the metal, some copper-toned alloy, worn smooth and discolored by touch.

With a little click, Helen opens the locket.

Inside, two portraits, similarly toned in gradations of black and white: on the left, their father, stolid but with a mischievous gleam in his eye, dapperly clad in his army uniform; on the right, their mother, a natural beauty, like Ruthie, too smart for her own good, a trait confirmed by an unmistakable sadness in the eyes.

Unable to help herself, Helen depresses the small dial near the clasp, and a softly tinny, darkly romantic tune, like one might hear from a miniature music box, begins to play. She holds the locket beneath her pillow, muffling the tune to the barely audible volume of a dream from which one has already woken up.

After a moment, the song slows and limps to a halt, landing on an unresolved note. Helen places a soft kiss on Ruthie's forehead, tucks the locket back into her hand, and goes to sleep.

...

The following morning arrives like a train, thrumming and ferocious in its clockwork precision. Hand in hand, Helen and Ruthie follow their guide—a professorial-looking editor named Henry—through the bowels of the *New Haven Herald*. With a clanking, industrial rhythm, a sea of whirring machines suck, chomp, and spit sheets of paper with violent alacrity. Henry, like the gravitational core of this little world, spreads his arms wide with a broad smile.

"Welcome to the *New Haven Herald*!"

Helen glances around at the hive of activity. Ruthie steels her posture, gripping Helen's hand like a security blanket. Henry, either oblivious to or uninterested in the girls' present state of grief-stricken distraction (and having presumably given the same tour dozens of times, on dozens of occasions), continues: "Obviously we wish you girls could join us under more cheerful circumstances, but we're quite pleased to have you. Right this way."

Henry leads Helen and Ruthie past rows upon rows of machinery: hulking presses, reams of wafer-thin paper, tables like butchers' slabs. Each wheel and knob is helmed by a child. Everywhere, smudges of ink glisten on youthful cheeks and tiny fingertips.

Ruthie presses herself against Helen's body as they walk. "Are they all orphans?" she whispers.

"I suppose so," Helen replies.

"Like us."

"No," Helen whispers back, injecting her tone with a touch of playful, sisterly camaraderie, "not like us. No one is like us."

Ruthie nearly smiles, the same sad almost-smile of their mother.

As Henry shepherds them through the space, Helen suddenly stops, her attention caught by a weathered-looking door. Above the frame, an inscription reads:

SCRIPTUM AETERNAM

"Ah, yes," Henry says. "That's where we keep the dead machines—antique

presses and so forth. It's mostly manned—or *womanned*, I should say—
by Clio." Henry waves to a bookish, raven-haired typesetter (evidently
Clio) on the opposite side of the room. She replies with a stilted nod
of the head. "She's obsessed with preserving language. Don't get her
started on Latin, Cornish, Magati Ke..."

But Helen's tenuous attention has strayed once again, this time as
Ruthie tugs the sleeve of her blouse. She follows Ruthie's gaze to an
abnormally tall, hauntingly gaunt janitor, his disproportionate features
exacerbated by a loose-fitting jumpsuit. He clutches a broom like a rifle,
dragging it swiftly and methodically downward against the debris-
strewn floor of the printing room. He looks up toward Ruthie and
Helen, as though feeling their stare, but his attempt at a smile manifests
as a brutish, toothy snarl.

"Don't mind Albert," says Henry, with the perfunctory gentility of
one for whom sympathy is exhausting. "He's a bit slow, essentially mute
but harmless. Keeps things clean for us." Helen's gaze drifts to Albert's
fingers, two of which are gorily avulsed and only partially healed.
"Terrible accident with a Linotype Simplex a few years back. Shame,
but dangerous machinery will do dangerous things. Any questions?"

Helen and Ruthie shake their heads. Henry smiles curtly.

"Good. Let's get you to work."

As sheets of paper glide from the maw of a printing press, Helen folds
them with numb alacrity. She stares down at her fingertips, now glazed
with thick, violet-black ink.

Beneath her fingertips, hundreds and hundreds of newspapers glow
with the day's headline: WAR OVER! VICTORY AT LAST!

Helen looks around, but there is no one with whom to share this
little irony. Her father has been killed in battle, barely a month before
the war's end. Now she, his orphaned daughter, will fold papers pro-
claiming the joy and triumph of the thing that killed him.

Her mother would certainly have appreciated the joke, however
grimly. Helen remembers her mother as a head more than anything: a

swath of dark hair and a beautiful brain into which momentary glimpses would be afforded, mostly in moments of humor. Her mother had an exceptionally marvelous laugh, but there was something dark and unfunny in it, a hint of melancholy or perhaps an even better joke that no one else had thought of. Helen wonders now if that was what made her laugh so marvelous.

Helen thinks of her mother, staring down at all the letters on the table, all addressed to the shifting outposts of the front lines. She remembers her mother's ink-stained fingers, stray tendrils of black seeping into the wood. And, of course, she remembers the last letter her mother ever wrote, the night she found out that all the other letters had been sent to a man who was already dead.

I am sorry.
I will be sorry forever.
All my love.—M

Helen and Ruthie hadn't found her, because the door to the cellar had been locked. The officer who broke down the door had said that this was a blessing, that they shouldn't have to see such a thing. But Helen couldn't fathom what seeing or not seeing mattered, when a thing was true either way. She had seen the fountain pen, cracked and slivered with blood, collected as evidence. That had been enough.

Her focus is jarred back to her fingertips by the sound of a warm, unfamiliar voice. "Ink gets everywhere working here." Helen looks up to see a fellow worker—handsome, dark-skinned, perhaps thirteen or fourteen—with that same pensive, stalwart smile of orphanhood. "I'm Dan."

Helen returns the smile. "I'm Helen."

Dan sets down a sheaf of freshly printed but unfolded papers. They shake hands, creases of skin and ink against creases of skin and ink. Dan nods toward Henry, stationed on the opposite side of the printing room. "Wild, isn't it?" he says.

At a distance, Helen watches as Henry presses a handkerchief to his nose and sneezes. As he lowers the handkerchief, she sees that it is speckled with blood . . . but the stain is not red. It's black.

That night, Helen lies awake again. She has been dreaming and sleeping and waking with little cognizance of which is which. She turns toward Ruthie, to see if she might be similarly afflicted . . . but the cot is empty.

Helen bolts upright, seizing the small lantern from beside the bed. She briefly considers waking Dan—her new and only friend—but thinks better of it.

Helen tiptoes past the army of sleeping children, and within moments, she is down the stairs, fumbling about for the entrance to the printing room. Now silent and inert, the printing room is an eerie wasteland of abandoned equipment. A haze of wintry light filters down through dust-glazed windows high above. Shadows fidget and yaw as Helen moves through the space, lantern trembling in her grasp, searching for any sign of Ruthie.

Passing a gamut of hulking machines, she approaches the ancient-looking door beneath the SCRIPTUM AETERNAM inscription. Now gaping like the mouth of a massive toy, the door is ajar.

With a sharp inhale, Helen gingerly steps through the doorway. Before her, a narrow hall—nearly cellar-like with its cold stone walls and downward slope—stretches outward toward oblivion. Helen peers into the darkness, willing her eyes to adjust. At the far end of the hall, a diminutive, dark silhouette—roughly Ruthie's size—hovers, sways, and darts past.

"Ruth? *Ruthie . . .*"

Leading with the quivering lantern, Helen steps cautiously down the hall. From somewhere—not far—the *THUMP THUMP THUMP* of metal on metal resounds in the darkness. As the sound grows louder, then louder still, Helen moves past the open doorway of a sepulchral, windowless chamber. Raising the lantern, she peeks inside: there, impossibly, a vintage Koenig & Bauer cylinder press roils on its own.

Helen takes a step back and nearly slips. She looks down . . .

The floor is a thick black sheen of ink.

Helen looks back toward the door to the printing room, now just a faint rectangle of moonlight, like the sky above an open grave.

She hesitates. Perhaps Ruthie was in the main room after all. Perhaps she had found a hiding place, then fallen asleep and hadn't heard Helen's voice or seen the lantern . . .

But Helen's reverie is interrupted by a familiar, unmistakable sound: Ruthie's locket. From somewhere deep within the network of halls, behind one of its doors, the jangling music box tune churns out its airy, slightly discordant melody . . . then suddenly stops.

Helen faces the closed door from behind which the sound seems to have come. It's marred by a set of violet-black fingerprints.

Mustering her courage, Helen pushes the door open with an agonizing creak . . .

"Ruthie?"

Only partly illumined by Helen's lantern, the room appears to be empty, save for a series of small black buckets. Helen shudders as something cold and thickly wet drips onto her cheek from above.

She lifts the lantern.

There, exactly like in her dream: swollen, skinned, and draining bodies, black with decay, hang and sway like wind chimes.

Helen screams, whirling toward the hall. But the floor is slick, and she skids into the unforgiving stone, cracking her head against the floor.

She slumps into the sheet of ink as she slips into unconsciousness.

Through a shadowy, dim-lit haze, Helen's eyes flicker open. She realizes, with her first glimmer of regained consciousness, that she is chained to the ancient cylinder press. The flat metal plates pump back and forth like the blade of a guillotine.

Clawing her way back into wakefulness, Helen begins to hyperventilate, thrashing violently against her restraints. With gnawing persistence, the blades of the machine inch toward her head . . .

At the edge of her field of vision, sinisterly half-lit by lamplight, Clio appears above her. She proffers a thin, long-suffering smile. "'Scriptum aeternam.' Do you know what that means? 'The written word lives forever.'" Clio draws a finger through her ink-black hair, then lightly strokes Helen's cheek. "Paper . . . ink . . . these elements make us immortal."

A curl of Helen's hair snags in the mechanism.

"Wouldn't you like to live forever, Helen?"

As Helen strains to extract her hair, one of her fingers is caught between the sliding sheets of metal, peeling the skin back from her finger like a glove. She cries out in anguish.

Suddenly, with a vicious *thwack*, wood on bone, Clio's head snaps to the side. She collapses against the edge of the machine, slicing a long, savage gash along her face and neck.

Behind her stands Albert, wielding his broom like a baseball bat. Moving quickly, he jams it into the mechanism, which promptly grinds to a halt. He scrambles to untie Helen from the machine, then tightly winds his handkerchief around the bleeding knob of her finger. With great difficulty, he stammers:

"Run."

Clio rises from the ground behind him like the undead monster she is. The gash extending along the side of her face and neck has gaped open to reveal not blood and bone, but a slithering, gelatinous mass of ink.

Dazed and desperate, Helen slides beneath Clio's arm and staggers into the hall. Clio jerks the broom handle free and pumps the pedal of the old Koenig & Bauer press, resuscitating the machine. As she grips Albert's throat and presses him downward, a thick spray of blood coats her skin.

Helen stumbles as quickly as she can through the pool of ink. Back in the hallway, she recovers her lantern, leaking oil but still burning, and presses toward the back of the hall. She screams: *"RUTH!"*

In response, a whimper emanates from somewhere nearby. Helen turns a corner and races toward the sound . . .

There, tucked into a catacomb-style alcove alongside a narrow, cracked, cobweb-laced window, is Ruthie, profoundly frightened but alive. Helen pulls her free and holds her close.

"What are you doing down here?"

Ruthie drags the back of her hand beneath her dripping nose and tear-dribbled cheeks. "I wanted to see the dead machines."

Setting this chilling bit of trivia aside for the moment, Helen looks around feverishly. There's no exit.

"Wait here, alright?"

Ruthie nods obediently. Helen gives her a swift kiss on the forehead, then inches her way slowly toward the main hall.

There, obscured by distance and patchy light, is Clio. As Helen watches, frozen to her stance as in a nightmare, the gruesome wound originating from Clio's neck widens further, then further, until the skin has fully peeled away to reveal a grisly, writhing ink monster. The creature is fast, fluid, somehow both skeletal and viscously wet...

As Clio rushes forward, Helen dashes the lantern on the ground. The floor, coated in ink, plumes into a blossom of flame.

Helen races toward the back wall and, awash with adrenaline, climbs into the catacomb-like nook in the wall alongside Ruthie. Moving her sister aside with an efficient embrace, Helen begins to violently kick at the narrow window. A sliver of a crack appears in the glass, then another. Behind them, barely audible over the crackling of the wildly growing fire, the writhing, undead mass of Clio can be heard slithering like a slug beneath salt, licks of black ink flashing through the now overlit darkness.

With a final, brutal kick to the window, Helen breaks through. A few more kicks, ribboning her ankles with blood, finish the job. She pulls Ruthie into her arms and forces her small body through the window. As a terrible screech emanates from the hall behind her, backed by the savage heartbeat rhythm of the cylinder press, she follows Ruthie through the jagged edges of the window.

As though waking from a dream, Helen and Ruthie emerge from the narrow opening onto a deserted, snow-flecked street. The lowermost row of windows blooms and pulses with fire, crawling upward toward the printing room and the sleeping barracks above. With a surge of relief, Helen spots Dan at the entrance, leading the children, sleepy and pajama-clad, to safety.

Helen looks down at her sister with a weak smile. But Ruth stares vacantly ahead, watching the building burn.

Helen drags her thumb beneath Ruth's nose. She frowns.

The blood is black, not red.

Years later, following a century of lore and restoration, the shell of the *New Haven Herald* building has been transformed into a clean, bright, Apollonian space. Industrial-grade printers and racks of large-format paper tumble and hum. The machines are no longer helmed by orphans (indeed, it's nearly impossible to believe that they ever were), and interns in khakis and polos—respectably aged eighteen instead of fifteen—weave among the shining metals and glossy grays of the contemporary press.

An elegant female guide wends her way through a gauntlet of cubicles, an eager young batch of interns on her heels. "Now, it's true we've been losing a lot of print to digital . . . but the old gods have a way of lingering." Above a metal and glass doorway, its lettering darkened and deepened by some long-forgotten fire, an inscription from the original press still looms, charred but extant: SCRIPTUM AETERNAM.

At the conclusion of her tour, the guide turns and smiles. Beneath a stylish crop of dark hair, a locket dangles around her neck, freckles of ink in the milgrain.

Ruth smiles.

"Welcome to the *New Haven Herald*."

Lacquer

WHEN THE BOTTLE of polish spills, a lagoon of Peach Side Babe No. 909 on hardwood, it is not only the shade of her toes but now the soles of her feet, carving rivulets in the skin of her heels and the pads beneath the toes, leaving ghosts of pink footprints en route to the kitchen. There, amid a junkyard of ceramics and utensils, beneath a spiral of light from the overhead bulb, she locates a towel. She has not consulted the literature, does not know whether the bar soap in the half shell on the edge of the sink will do the trick. She will clean through the night, not because of the polish but because now, on her knees, she sees it is already a disaster—flecks of plaster and hair, crumbs and dust and detritus of unspecified origin. She will see herself in the mirror, amid the half loaf of bread and the candlesticks from Spain and the cup with the chip and the towels that should really be replaced, the needles and thread and waffle iron and flat iron and from her vantage on the floor, it looks as though she is holding all these things aloft, a caryatid of unwelcome history. She will finish her work, extinguish the bulb, and tread back to the bedroom, slick with error, over a floor that has never been so clean.

The Train Speaks

"THIS IS A BLUE LINE train to 7th Street, Metro Center."

He has always believed in poetry. He also believes in irony, but he is not sure this qualifies.

"Don't forget to take your belongings," he tells himself.

He thinks of the silent movie actors, stilted ghosts, up to their antics for as long as the reels survive. Having traded the cellular for the celluloid, the rude seven-year turnover of skin cells for the longevity of film.

"Now arriving: Willow Street Station. The next stop is Wardlow Station."

He earnestly entreats himself not to eat, drink, or smoke on trains or on platforms. To keep his feet off the seats. (Please.)

He is impressed by the ubiquity. Many people are. He is in many places at once. Ignored. Like God.

116 · *The Train Speaks*

He listens for anything else. The antique grind of the rails, the labored breathing of the ventilation system, the dull wobble of the sides against the wind of the tunnel. The water torture dinging of texts.

Feet are on seats, everywhere.

"Now arriving: Vernon Station. The next stop is Washington Station."

His mother visited, once, bounding forth from the Southwest arrivals terminal with the compact, white-hot, mistaken energy of a thousand suns.

He had suggested hiring a car (he had proudly carved his check from the Metro voiceover job into roughly a hundred twenties and hidden these around his studio, like a childhood Easter egg hunt, so it was sort of fiscally viable), but she had insisted upon hearing his voice, so they boarded a bus to the nearest train station. Some other voice, perky and sterile like a robot, had greeted them. His mother had twisted her mouth into an angular, coat-hanger curl of distaste, giddily itching for the main event.

He recalls the way she had stood in the underground lobby of Wilshire/Normandie, fixed like a wax figurine, studying the sallow fluorescent glow of the system map. Framed in a latticework of delicate graffiti, she had traced the thick, blood-red aorta of the line to Hollywood, the limp, dangling blue vena cava chugging upward from Long Beach.

"Now arriving: Pico Station. The next stop is 7th Street, Metro Center."

He beseeches himself to please be considerate to those around him. To refrain from playing loud music. To please, seriously, absolutely not eat under any circumstances while aboard the train, for the love of God.

He thumbs the fossil-hard edge of a mash of gum on the seat fabric, oddly offended.

He thanks everyone, magnanimously, for going Metro.

"This is the last stop. Please make sure to take your belongings, and exit the train at this time."

He exits the train, per his instruction. He remembers what it was like to be commanding. Thankful. Certain. How could he forget?

"For your personal safety, do not sit or stand near the edge of the platform."

Surging with the thrill of insurrection, he strides to the edge of the platform, his heels just beyond the fat yellow line meant to keep wayward passengers at bay.

"Please stand clear. The doors are closing."

He thinks of his mother, folded into a neat, deflated shell, thumbing a Neolithic gum wad on the adjacent seat. "Why carpet?" she had asked.

"I'm not sure," he had said.

He peers down the tunnel, a great concrete throat, the rails laid out like vertebrae.

He knows what they will say. What he will say.

"We apologize for the delay."

He thinks of the silent film actresses, strapped to the rails, thrashing about with the implausible sangfroid of a 100 percent survival rate. He thinks of their shining, grateful faces. He wonders where they're buried.

"We appreciate your patience," he'll say.

He sticks his head out. No drama. Minds the gap like a surgeon.

As the doors slide closed, he welcomes everyone, everywhere at once.

The light appears at the end of the tunnel.

And he hears nothing.

Picking the Wound

SHE MONITORS THE opalescent Tic Tac of a scar like the first-time owner of a desert plant, standoffish and anxiety-ridden.

Each morning, with the precision of clockwork, the curvature of her ankle bleeds like a waterfall, a Tarantinan-Elizabethan deluge of blood, inevitable and inexorable.

The phone rings, again. The display reads DREAM GIRL, an alert hyperbolized by the tinny glissando of a mawkish ringtone.

She mops up the blood with her whitest towel, like a moron. Waves of red lap at the pocky hardwood, wet and indifferent. Through the excitement, fingers of panic claw their way up her aorta. She fantasizes about cleaning up some fabulous, more serious crime.

Between calls, the silence festers like a blister—best left alone, impossible to ignore.

Rinsing the towel, she thinks: *This is RED*. She cross-checks the towel against her ninety-six-pack of Crayolas and discovers that it's more like Bittersweet. Possibly Brick Red.

She reads up on the anterior tibial artery, the posterior tibial artery, so recently, recurrently ruptured by her negligence. She considers whether she'll do it again, contemplates her next shower with the splanchnic, sickly sweet feeling of staring downward from a height.

Dream Girl stops calling. (This, of course, is to be expected.) She feels the thrill of having done this, having put to death an entire alternate reality.

She scours a very long article about the ankle-brachial index, courtesy of the Mayo Clinic, but is betrayed by its irrelevance.

She takes a walk, up and over, block by block, listing slightly to the left (to accommodate the wound), toward one particular upper-story window where the lights switch on and off with disciplined, enviable regularity. Somewhere above, Dream Girl looms like a ghost, omnipotent and immaterial, beneath a wash of Ikea lighting.

Four stories below, the cotton rim of her sock plumes in a blossom of Bittersweet (possibly Brick Red) blood.

She limps. Conjures magnitude. Takes credit for the failure of her tools, a most excellent carpenter.

She wishes, intently, for everything to mean something, but must admit that this means nothing. That sometimes one is simply terrible at shaving.

It is unlikely that she will try a different type of blade, or alter the angle at which she shaves the doomed swerve at the base of her calf.

She will, instead, glide the tip of her nail beneath the scab, and invite the wound again.

Totenhaus

HERR KÖHLER IS A handsome man, all jaw, rigorous cloud-gray eyes that darken and mist as he speaks of his wife. Frau Köhler—the object of his sorrow—lies in an elegant, parable-caliber state of repose on the stretcher beside him. She is a lithe, fragile, mythic beauty, exquisitely inert. Her skin is nearly translucent, speckled with vivid purple, blood-rushed bruises.

"A carriage accident," Herr Köhler explains.

"Of course," Herr Schwartz replies with a polished, cooing sympathy, as though a carriage could leave thumbprints beneath the jaw.

As the two men stare with longing at the lost life beneath them, as though she was ever anything other than lost, I feel what I have always felt in this place: that I am an interloper, a hundred-pound fly on the wall, a voyeur.

This place is, after all, a Totenhaus.

A house of the dead.

Death is a tricky thing at this moment in time. Science and medicine have never been more compelling, but there have also been an excess of slip-ups—nail marks discovered on the insides of coffins, bodies suddenly bolting upright, half-desiccated, on the mortician's slab. Struck by a plague of taphephobia, several of the most prominent German families have hauled their dearly departed to the Totenhaus, a kind of waiting room, jammed with flowers, where the bodies of the deceased (or not) are laid for a period to ensure that they are, in fact, deceased prior to burial.

Of course, in the event that a body is, in fact, not deceased, someone must be there to greet them, to assure them that they are not mad, to alert their loved ones and to protect them from the fate of Juliet awaking in the crypt.

This, since my relocation from Paris, where I have seen a number of things worse than death, has been my profession.

La Terreur—the Reign of Terror—has the glamorous historical ring of having been terribly, viciously loud. And it was, of course—those roaring, undulating crowds, the slick whir and crunch of the guillotines. But more than anything, I remember the terror as silence, aftermath. The emptiness of the streets, the absolute quiet. The bodies outnumbering the grave plots, and a kind of whisper in the trees: *Enterre moi . . . Enterre moi . . .*

Bury me.

There is nothing irregular, nothing macabre, about a single dead body. But when several dead bodies slump together, clumped and fused in a tangle of limbs, and float down the Seine like a raft . . . this is when one begins to fear death.

I am not mad; I have worked with the living. I was a nurse (once). But in the wake of revolution (la révolution), a parade of death so casual and purposeful, all I can see is the almost-death of any person, their innate tragic flaws—the cough, the wound—that will slowly unravel and sever the cord.

There's a kind of dull and swollen boredom to being surrounded by death, like watching paint dry, if paint were the blood in the veins or the plump, damp luster of the skin. It is certain and slow, underwhelming and inexorable.

My diet has become borderline biblical, dominated by bread and wine (with a ratio tipped heavily toward the latter). But the key to a sense of calm, a comfort with the sepulchral residents of das Totenhaus, is to add just a touch of embalming fluid to one's glass of wine. The sensation is at once poison and preservation, the banal pace of eternity, a taste of knowing everything and thus profoundly not caring.

Death purportedly dissolves marriages, so Frau Köhler is technically no longer Frau Köhler; she is now (again, pre– and post–Herr Köhler) simply Ingrid. I imagine her skin, paper-thin and eager, taking to his like a graft. In the event that she awakes—a thing that has never happened in this purgatorial living-room mausoleum—he will be notified. He will be surprised.

He visits sporadically, hovers over her corpse with a tight, watchful focus. It is unclear what he expects from these little visits.

Her stretcher is nestled between two similar contraptions, occupied by two of the more attractive corpses, near the window, where a glaze of semi-regular sunlight casts a bleak sheen over her delicate features. The gaping front window, sheathed in an ashy lace curtain, is something of a standing dare among the local youths. Peeking is routine, and this artful casting of bodies will ideally deter (or, less ideally, complicate) the nightmares of boys aged thirteen to fifteen.

From the moment of her arrival, Ingrid is bathed in magic. There are fifty-four bodies in the tight little room; she is fifty-five—fünfundfünfzig. From a certain angle, her body bleeds into the bouquets of das Schleierkraut—baby's breath—and appears as a small, isolated lump of undulating flowers.

· · ·

By the fifth day, Ingrid's bruises have begun to heal. Like magic. On either side of her, the stiff, buxom corpse of a thirty-eight-year-old woman and the brittle limbs of a twelve-year-old girl have started to blacken and swell. But Ingrid is intact. The violet, bead-like wounds around her throat have begun to dissipate.

Dead bodies, of course, tend not to heal.

So I do what any normal person would do. I go to the kitchen, draw a rusted knife from its sheath, return to the room of the dead, and delve the tip of the knife into the gap between her first two toes. I draw the blade downward to the crest of her heel. A plume of thick, viscous red blood leaks from her foot.

I breathe a sigh comprised of equal parts disappointment and relief. She is dead.

As the sun sets, I am alone with the bodies. When I first began, I initially tried filling the void by singing—

> Sieben Jahr
> Trüb und klar
> Hänschen in der Fremde war.
> Da besinnt
> Sich das Kind,
> Eilt nach Haus geschwind.
> Doch nun ist's kein Hänschen mehr.

but when I learned the meaning of the German lyrics, a child who had vanished and never returned home, I stopped. No song sounded right, sung to this massive audience, deaf and endlessly attentive.

I go to the kitchen, where I make a show (for no one other than myself) of selecting a wineglass, though in the end I will drink from the bottle. I pour in a dram of embalming fluid—das Gift, an expression that means "present" in English and "poison" in German. Never has a flourish of etymology seemed more splendidly or aptly ironic.

I drink deeply, feeling the cocky adrenaline of being alive, and the haunting thrill of proximity to death. A shift in heart rate. The lavish glow of nausea and sweat, a swimming of the senses. A sensitivity to the old house's pipe system, which chugs with a musical rhythm:

Enterre moi . . . Enterre moi . . .

I am jarred from my reverie by the loud, bright ringing of a bell.

This is always frightening, and nearly always normal. There are fifty-five bells in the Totenhaus, each hung from the ceiling and strung to the finger of its respective corpse. These are designed to alert me, the watchperson, to a body that is actually alive. But as anyone who has served as watchperson in a house of the dead knows, the dead move frequently. Bodies shift, curl, seize, deflate. Because I wish to see none of these things, am no longer curious or hopeful, I wait, braced against the kitchen table, drinking das Gift, and wait for the ringing to stop.

But it does not stop.

Another bell rings, then another, and another, and another, until the entire adjacent room is rattling with a cacophony of bells.

I drop the bottle, which shatters at my feet. As the ringing grows and swells in volume, a kind of chorus emerges: *Enterre moi . . . Enterre moi . . .*

But this is, of course, all in my mind. Has to be. I laugh, aloud. Too loudly. These bodies do not speak French. If it were real, I would hear *Begrabe mich.*

The voice is soft, feminine, strained.

I jerk open a drawer and seize a butcher's knife. From the next room, a blur of candlelight shifts and wanes.

The bells stop.

Flush with the feeling of omniscience—an all-knowing and not-wanting-to-know—I step softly toward the room of the dead.

All is as it ought to be, save for the listless dangling of the disturbed bells.

But one cot is empty.

Ingrid is gone.

Carving a ragged pathway along the floor, a series of lines—the strip of blood from her cut heel—marks a staggering curve toward the upper stair.

The dead, apparently, walk.

The gaping front window, protectively barred, is open. There's no room for a body (either ingress or egress), but a breeze has begun to extinguish the candles, throwing the room into a dull, ethereal darkness. Moonlight pools against the gaunt clavicles and corroding pores of the dead.

There is a kind of horror to the absence of demons, the placid, black silence. No conflict, no objection. Merely death on death.

I look toward the front door—clear safety, obvious retreat. But I am understanding, finally, that there's a reason that the tree of knowledge was the undoing of humankind. I am bored, and curious, and need, above all, to know. Which is why, inevitably, the wisest among us go up the stairs.

Each step is marred with a parallel stripe of blood, and each step creaks with a whining, percussive rhythm: *Begrabe mich . . . Begrabe mich . . .*

The candlelight from the room where the bodies are laid, like a graveyard pushed upward to the surface of earth, glimmers and dims. The door at the top of the stairs gapes, broad and black, the door flung open, freckles of blood on the banister. Each stair step is a vertebra, leading to the place where a head ought to be.

After what feels like an eternity, I reach the landing.

There, a slat-roofed attic stretches in every direction, amorphously framed by leaking shadows.

I step across the floor—*Begrabe mich . . . Begrabe mich . . .*—but the space is empty. I walk toward the curve of an unused balcony as the wind catches the door and slams it shut behind me.

My head swims. Needles prick the lining of my stomach; fingers of panic claw their way up my lungs. Human forms—intertwined and indistinct, like a cluster of bodies in the Seine—cloud my vision. I walk toward the sliver of light at the edge of the room.

There, braced against the rail of the balcony like the figurehead at the prow of a ship, is Ingrid. She turns.

"Es gibt Dinge, die schlimmer sind als der Tod."

There are things worse than death.

"Ich kenne," I say.

I know.

I would carry her downstairs, to what must have felt like a hospital when she awoke. But before I can move, her body sinks like a stone, a flutter of cloth and skin, to the earth below. She hits the ground with a sickening whir and crunch, the snapping of bones, reminiscent of a guillotine.

In the morning, Herr Köhler will come to visit. He will study Ingrid, this splay of pale limbs and fresh bruises, silently puzzling at her wounds.

And left alone, quietly poised in a flicker of candlelight, I will sit awake, praying that the wounds do not heal.

Retrospect

A SIGN APPEARS above the shop on 14th Street: BEAUTY IS IN
THE EYE.

We laugh when it's installed. Beyond the comically quaint storefront,
the antiquated clapboards, and the aforementioned sign swinging idly
from the awning, one can see clearly, through the smeared glass of the
front window, that the interior is empty. Weeds sprout from the cracked
concrete floor. Ivy trickles down the walls at odd angles. At the center
of the space, a gaping rift in the concrete glows with the embers of an
unattended campfire. The roof, of all things, is simply absent. (Was
there a roof before? Surely there must have been.)

We are united in our eye-rolling, our smirks. We are not so much
disturbed as amused.

There's something rustic, nostalgic even, about the scent of the camp-fire that wafts through town at all hours. Something magical about its glow, half-obscured by the fountain at the center of the square.

Over the coming weeks, our amusement shifts to annoyance, then, gradually, curiosity. More and more people enter and exit the shop, ostensibly to see what all the fuss is about. They emerge in one of two ways: scoffing and guffawing, typically within moments of entry, or hours later, gazing up toward the sky like a baby seeing its first balloon.

More weeks pass. The sky, tinged with smoke, edges from blue to light blue, then a drained shade of white-gray. Farmlands curl into dry, barren patches of bald earth, although the farmers seem inexplicably pleased. The forest around town grows withered and gnarled, pale with the first signs of decay. "The season," we say. "The winter. That's all."

People go missing, and there's a kind of charm to the mystery. These same people are found, at unpredictable intervals, in odd poses about town. Lounging in the home of a rival, confident that it's their home. At the local hall, giving a lecture on a topic about which they know nothing. Splayed (just that once) in an outline of blood, arms spread wide, as though having fallen while attempting to fly.

Curiosity festers and gnaws, claws and swells, until one day, I visit the shop. Outside the entrance, two women are hunched, cooing, over a mongrel nibbling the limb of a dessicated, unidentifiable animal. "How beautiful," one of them says softly.

I enter the shop and, almost instantly, as though a bell had been rung, the shop owner appears. He's astonishingly dapper, suit-clad, with all the trappings of a typical shop owner. He smiles conspiratorially. "Here to see what the fuss is all about?"

I feel myself blush. Why lie? "Yes," I say, "Why else?"

The shopkeeper tilts his head toward the fire. "What do you see?" he asks.

"Fire," I say.

He laughs. "And what do you *wish* to see?"

I stare into the fire. Here, from the inside, the wall-crawling ivy, laced with shadows, makes sense. The sky above is breathtaking. (Why have we ever had roofs?) The flames lap and lull with a kind of low-slung genius.

"I wish to see things as they were," I hear myself say. I surge with embarrassment, but the shopkeeper smiles.

"Expensive," he says, "but worth it."

He guides me to a storeroom at the back of the shop, converted to a minuscule clinic. Above a cloth-covered cot, a trio of surgical lamps is perched, nimble and elegant as long-necked birds.

In answer to a question I haven't yet asked, I'm handed a menu. Prices are listed, in escalating order, alongside a smattering of items:

> More handsome husband.
> Well-behaved child.
> Good weather.
> Prosperity.

"Magic, I know," says the shopkeeper, as though he, too, is chagrined by the premise.

I sit on the edge of the cot, dizzy from the smoke.

"People see what they want to see," he continues. "In a sense, this is merely a formality." He scoots a slick white device toward my head. "Simple laser eye surgery," he says, and through the lens, I can see a wealth of glass reflected on glass. A kaleidoscope of possibility. At center, the laser, warning-red.

"When were you thinking?" he asks, attentive and casual as if he were asking my favorite ice cream flavor.

"When things were good," I hear myself say.

He nods, and I can see in this nod that I'm not the first to have said this.

"Open your eyes for me," he says.

In the weeks to come, I am stunned by the beauty of the world. The sky has never been so blue, the water so clear. Neighbors who seemed moronic are suddenly sensical, not obese but robust, gracefully aging into strong opinions and the splendor of prestige.

Sounds, occasionally, are odd. I wake, one night, to the sound of sirens, but am relieved to find not a crime scene but a parade. In the morning, there are bodies on the pavement, still, presumably, passed out from the festivities.

Weeks pass. There are more parades than usual.

I'm delighted for the happiness of the populace, respectful of the partygoers passed out in the square each morning. I'm thrilled by the appearance of roses, violently red, planted in unexpected splotches and tendrils throughout the square. I'm puzzled but unfazed when the roses are cleared each morning.

Nonetheless, despite the air of festivity, there is something to be said for peace and quiet.

I make my way to the edge of town, past the drained fountain, the closed shops (owners on holiday, no doubt), where the forest has grown more verdant than ever. Here—I remember from childhood—there's a cornfield that produces the most perfect, succulent corn. As of now (on account of the season), it's flat and lush with grass, green as an emerald, struck through with stones roughly two feet high—markers, no doubt, of where the various corn strains will go.

I sit at the edge of the field, breathing the cleanest air imaginable, beneath a sky brighter, bluer than it's ever been, and wait for the corn to grow.

Year of the Snake

1989

Chùsi is ten today, double digits, an achievement marked by the coming-of-age sacrament of frybread with sprinkles and icing for breakfast. Cupcakes are scheduled for three o'clock, but Chùsi got what she came for.

This is the year of the brick-by-brick dismantling of the Soviet Bloc, the ascent of Václav Havel, and Chùsi's pronouncement, for the first and only time, of her aspiration to become a professional roller skater. The coming years will be rife with disillusionment regarding the prospects of a career in roller skating—to say nothing of the ideological affinity between East and West—but today these things are irrefutable.

Chùsi drapes herself over the rail of the penguin habitat, propped on the rubber toe stop of her size 3 white Chicago Rollers like a pro. Her legs, precariously long, shiver with the chill of shipped-in ice, the glinting heat of an eternal San Diego June.

A few yards off, a khaki-slacked guide delivers a careful, sweeping monologue about the tundra biome to a coterie of tourists, none of whom has given any indication of understanding English. They peer from beneath sun visors in every direction, but primarily upward, where members of the zoo staff balance on ladders, winding streamers over the stumpy limbs of faux baobab trees. Chùsi watches, mesmerized, as though witnessing an act of suburban vandalism transpire in slow motion.

"Decorations for the annual gala," the guide explains. He launches into a brief lecture on permafrost, and then, because no one is listening, he says, "The zoo, ladies and gentlemen. A shrine to anthropocentrism."

From his perch atop one of the ladders, a zoo employee, arms laden with crepe paper, looks down at Chùsi, a thing she feels before she sees. The moment is nothing until her mother steps beside her, overtly close—the instinctive, violently watchful posture of a mother lioness.

Chùsi rolls along the pathway, away from her mother, from the man.

At one o'clock, Chùsi's father will be joining them for birthday lunch at the Olive Garden, and as she shuffles toward the reptile pavilion, Chùsi tries to focus on what she will order. She is suddenly aware of her salmon pink terry cloth shorts, her thin, tanned arms. She hates her skates, though it is hard to say why. Later, at lunch, she will ask her father what *anthropocentrism* means. He will know.

As the pathway slopes into shade, Chùsi braces herself against the rail amid a gallery of plexiglass rectangles, each box a slithering tableau. She fixates on a placard describing the tiger snake, *Notechis scutatus*. Chùsi, at ten, finds this hilarious, the premise of an animal named after another animal. A thing masquerading as another thing.

She wonders if the snake is fooled, graceful and fixed as a ballerina in a music box, by the limp, verdant plants in its two-by-two-foot plastic cube.

She wonders if it was young enough, when it first arrived, to believe that this is the size of the world.

2001

Mildly inebriated and infinitely bored, Chùsi gazes upward through a constellation of Christmas lights. A massive improvement over the chintzy streamers of yore.

It is June, and the world surges with the scot-free thrill of having outwitted Y2K. Chùsi is twenty-two and cloaked in magic, the chosen emissary of an effort by the Old Globe Theater to concurrently resurrect Shakespeare and raise money for the Elephant Odyssey exhibit. How these two things could possibly be connected is unclear, but the initiative seems to be propelled by high-cheekboned, ethnically ambiguous youth and a nebulous zeal for the finer things.

As Chùsi takes a delicate, focused pull from her cranberry vodka—the first drink she's learned to order—a resentfully handsome, bow-tied emcee announces her. Chùsi Chen. Chùsi's agent has convinced her to hold on to her real name like a life raft. Chùsi had made a joke about *white*water rafting with an exotic name, but the agent had stared blankly, as if to say *I make the jokes around here*.

Chùsi ascends the stage, a vision in floor-length gold, the texture of half-wet nail polish. She has seen the way this audience looks at the animals. She throbs with this feeling—the sensation of worship, the lent power of being adored.

Chùsi speaks:

> I am fire and air; my other elements
> I give to baser life. So; have you done?
> Come then, and take the last warmth of my lips . . .

She kisses the air, feeling at once majestic and profoundly silly.

If thou and nature can so gently part,
The stroke of death is as a lover's pinch,
Which hurts, and is desired . . .

She presses an imaginary asp to her breast.

With thy sharp teeth this knot intrinsicate
Of life at once untie: poor venomous fool
Be angry, and dispatch . . .

Chùsi dies on stage, grandly, then bows beneath a halo of lights, unfazed by the tenuous causality between a four-hundred-year-old play and saving the animals. They will write checks, this sea of pocketbooks and suit jackets, and she will have been part of it, touched by the tumid thrill of casual largess. She, too, will save the elephants tonight.

In the shadowy corridor of the Reptile Walk, the order of rectangles has changed a bit; upgrades to the plant life are visible—the result, no doubt, of the proceeds from preceding galas. Still, the tiger snake is not difficult to find.

From behind her, a slurred interjection: "You're Chùsi Chen."

Chùsi turns and smiles a deterrent smile. But he is not deterred, this middle-aged heir in a garish leopard-print smoking jacket, gesticulating with a martini like a prosthetic limb.

"I liked your Cleopatra." He sways toward her, the martini glass dipping precariously in his grasp. His eyes rove over her cheekbones, her mouth.

"What are you?"

Chùsi smiles, a taught smile. "I'm an actor. And a philanthropist tonight, like everyone."

"No, what *are* you? Ethnically, I mean."

"Half Native American, half Chinese," she says, an admission that feels like unbuttoning the top button of one's blouse, not intending to.

"How did *that* happen?"

"My mother had unprotected sex with my father."

The man laughs, the laugh of someone clever enough to have commissioned this joke. "I was like, *in what war?*"

Chùsi fixates on the man's Adam's apple, a flimsy gyro wheel bouncing with his laughter, tugging against the paper-thin tissue of his throat.

"I saw you in that film. The one with the robots. You were very good."

"Thank you," she says, not knowing what she is supposed to be thankful for. Her gaze shifts back to the snake in its cage, an object of cramped, impeded dignity.

As Chùsi fixes her gaze on the serpent, the man leans forward, his scent both damply corny and expensive.

"Do you know who I am?"

"No."

He snorts a laugh. "You would kill to get my business card."

Chùsi laughs. She would not kill for his or any business card.

"Chùsi Chen," the man says again. And when Chùsi does not react, he sneers and exhales, a haze of alcohol and heat, then vanishes with a flourish of imagined triumph.

Chùsi watches the tiger snake, its golden belly etched in slivers of charcoal.

And then, for no other reason than that she is partly drunk and has always wanted to, she steps toward the unmarked employee door that looks like a seam-hinged stone. The slab folds inward onto an orange-lit hallway, a basic, unmagical tunnel of doors and buckets and latches.

With an unhurried certitude, Chùsi unlatches the door to the tiger snake's cage.

The creature glides and sniffs around the edge of the opening. Then, like a drop of molasses, the snake slides across the threshold, a gaping invitation, and descends into a graceful curl on the floor.

Chùsi returns to the party, blushing with the elite thrill of crime without repercussion. The man in the leopard-print jacket haunts the bar beside his wife, a blossom of hair above a patchwork of hard edges and unyielding curves.

Beneath the tinkling, tittering sounds of civilization are the scents of earth, of sweat and hide, of the world as it has always been.

2013

Chùsi has visited the zoo only once in the past decade, shortly after receiving her license as an EMT. A suicidal visitor had climbed into the Northern Frontier, hoping to invite some mortal violence from either the polar bears or the caribou, but had slipped and fallen into the arctic pool before being whisked off to Scripps Mercy to be treated for a humiliating, nonfatal case of hypothermia.

Chùsi has given up acting, the latest in a string of not-quite-careers. She has seen the world stretch and curl against its stitches, rejecting its wounds, healing oddly.

It is now June, and Chùsi slips through the gala, lit by a pulse of red and blue, with the finesse of an unrecognized god. The attendees part like water, a muted rustle of unlikely fabrics.

Overhead, Chinese paper lanterns swing from the trees like phosphorescent corpses, likely recycled from last year's gala. The Year of the Dragon.

The patient—a snakebite victim—is transferred to the stretcher, her ankle budding with a bloated, blackening bruise. Aside from this flaw, she is a paragon of splendidly molded limbs and symmetrical features.

Chùsi presses the stretcher toward the glow of the ambulance. From behind her, a slurred interjection: "Thank you for saving my wife."

It is the man from twelve years before, the martini-armed cyborg. It's a new wife, of course, the former presumably lying around somewhere like so much shed skin.

As the doors of the ambulance are flung open, the man's eyes drift to the rod of Aeschylus, the serpent coiled around its staff, stitched above her breast. He reaches behind a zebra-print pocket square and presses a business card into her palm, saying, "That's my direct line."

As the doors of the ambulance swing closed, Chùsi fits a BVM over the patient's mouth. She listens for the languid seethe of oxygen while her partner—a "former barista, future doctor," as he likes to say—rifles through an onboard collection of anti-venom medication. The patient's blood shoves itself along the veins beneath a crepe paper sheath of skin, slugging toward the taut, violet-gray bulb of the snakebite.

Framed by the glass of the rear doors, the party recedes from foreground to background, a hub of light amid a shroud of constructed wilderness. The guests hunch in elegant postures of worry, then slowly break off and mill about, testing the mood. Around them, unseen but felt, animals stir like phantoms in the dark.

Chùsi fingers the business card, etching a light, insistent rectangle against the skin through her pocket.

It will be a very good year.

ACKNOWLEDGMENTS

I'M GRATEFUL FOR the support of a number of extraordinary publications with which these stories found first homes, including *Boulevard* ("Obscure Trivia of the Antarctic"), *Story* ("Octopus"), *Columbia Journal* ("Casualty"), *Stories of the Nature of Cities* ("Ori Dreams of a Tree"), *Chicago Quarterly Review* ("All the Places You Will Never Be Again"), *The Offing* ("Insertion"), *Iron Horse Literary Review* ("Cain vs. Cain"), *Gertrude Press* ("The Body Electric"), *Lunch Ticket* ("Eating the Leaves"), *Chicago Review* ("Mnemophobe"), *Sunspot* ("Lacquer"), *Oxford Magazine* ("The Train Speaks"), *Moon City Review* ("Picking the Wound"), *Black Static* ("Totenhaus"), *Epiphany* ("Retrospect"), and the *Masters Review* ("Year of the Snake"). Pieces of this collection were developed with the generous support of the Alpine Fellowship Foundation (original publisher of "The Lady Will Pay for Everything"), the Banff Centre, the Cambridge Writers' Workshop, the Wellstone Center in the Redwoods, Bethany Arts Community, and the Hudson Valley Writers Center.

Creating a book entails far more than simply writing it, and I'm deeply grateful to those who did the serious work. Many thanks to the remarkable team at University of Iowa Press, including director James McCoy, associate director and exceptional designer Karen Copp, tireless and gifted editors Susan Hill Newton and Lori Paximadis, and marketing director Allison Means, without whose efforts you probably wouldn't be reading this. Thanks also to Anthony Marra, whose extraordinary generosity as a writer is fortunately matched by his generosity as a reader.

I am especially grateful to my mother, who taught me to read and write, and who edited multiple stories in this collection before her death. It's hard to imagine how good the other stories would be if she were still around. I'm also very grateful to my father, whose gifts of humor and reinvention shine through my better work. He, too, would have loved this collection, I think, even if he didn't totally understand it. To my brother, Daniel, a good man, whose patience for vetting adjectives has occasionally proven valuable. And, more than anyone, to Joshua, my partner, the sort of person you can't write about, because they're too good to be believable.

THE IOWA SHORT FICTION AWARD AND THE
JOHN SIMMONS SHORT FICTION AWARD WINNERS,
1970–2022

Lee Abbott
Wet Places at Noon
Cara Blue Adams
You Never Get It Back
Donald Anderson
Fire Road
Dianne Benedict
Shiny Objects
A. J. Bermudez
*Stories No One Hopes Are
about Them*
Marie-Helene Bertino
Safe as Houses
Will Boast
Power Ballads
David Borofka
Hints of His Mortality
Robert Boswell
Dancing in the Movies
Mark Brazaitis
*The River of Lost Voices:
Stories from Guatemala*

Jack Cady
The Burning and Other Stories
Jennine Capó Crucet
How to Leave Hialeah
Pat Carr
The Women in the Mirror
Kathryn Chetkovich
Friendly Fire
Cyrus Colter
The Beach Umbrella
Marian Crotty
What Counts as Love
Jennifer S. Davis
Her Kind of Want
Janet Desaulniers
What You've Been Missing
Sharon Dilworth
The Long White
Susan M. Dodd
Old Wives' Tales
Merrill Feitell
Here Beneath Low-Flying Planes

Christian Felt
The Lightning Jar
James Fetler
Impossible Appetites
Starkey Flythe Jr.
Lent: The Slow Fast
Kathleen Founds
*When Mystical Creatures
Attack!*
Sohrab Homi Fracis
*Ticket to Minto: Stories of
India and America*
H. E. Francis
The Itinerary of Beggars
Abby Frucht
Fruit of the Month
Tereze Glück
*May You Live in
Interesting Times*
Ivy Goodman
Heart Failure
Barbara Hamby
Lester Higata's 20th Century
Edward Hamlin
*Night in Erg Chebbi and
Other Stories*
Ann Harleman
Happiness
Elizabeth Harris
The Ant Generator
Ryan Harty
*Bring Me Your Saddest
Arizona*

Charles Haverty
Excommunicados
Mary Hedin
*Fly Away Home: Eighteen
Short Stories*
Beth Helms
American Wives
Jim Henry
*Thank You for Being
Concerned and Sensitive*
Allegra Hyde
Of This New World
Matthew Lansburgh
Outside Is the Ocean
Lisa Lenzo
Within the Lighted City
Kathryn Ma
*All That Work and Still
No Boys*
Renée Manfredi
Where Love Leaves Us
Susan Onthank Mates
The Good Doctor
John McNally
Troublemakers
Molly McNett
One Dog Happy
Tessa Mellas
Lungs Full of Noise
Kate Milliken
If I'd Known You Were Coming
Kevin Moffett
Permanent Visitors

Lee B. Montgomery
Whose World Is This?
Rod Val Moore
Igloo among Palms
Lucia Nevai
Star Game
Thisbe Nissen
*Out of the Girls' Room
and into the Night*
Dan O'Brien
Eminent Domain
Janice Obuchowski
The Woods
Philip F. O'Connor
*Old Morals, Small
Continents, Darker Times*
Robert Oldshue
November Storm
Eileen O'Leary
Ancestry
Sondra Spatt Olsen
Traps
Elizabeth Oness
Articles of Faith
Lon Otto
A Nest of Hooks
Natalie L. M. Petesch
*After the First Death There
Is No Other*
Marilène Phipps-Kettlewell
*The Company of Heaven:
Stories from Haiti*

Glen Pourciau
Invite
C. E. Poverman
The Black Velvet Girl
Michael Pritchett
The Venus Tree
Nancy Reisman
House Fires
Josh Rolnick
Pulp and Paper
Sari Rosenblatt
Father Guards the Sheep
Blake Sanz
The Boundaries of Their Dwelling
Elizabeth Searle
My Body to You
Enid Shomer
Imaginary Men
Chad Simpson
Tell Everyone I Said Hi
Heather A. Slomski
*The Lovers Set Down
Their Spoons*
Marly Swick
A Hole in the Language
Barry Targan
*Harry Belten and the
Mendelssohn Violin Concerto*
Annabel Thomas
The Phototropic Woman
Jim Tomlinson
Things Kept, Things Left Behind

Douglas Trevor
*The Thin Tear in the Fabric
of Space*
Laura Valeri
The Kind of Things Saints Do
Anthony Varallo
This Day in History
Ruvanee Pietersz Vilhauer
*The Water Diviner and
Other Stories*
Don Waters
Desert Gothic
Lex Williford
Macauley's Thumb

Miles Wilson
Line of Fall
Russell Working
Resurrectionists
Emily Wortman-Wunder
Not a Thing to Comfort You
Ashley Wurzbacher
Happy Like This
Charles Wyatt
Listening to Mozart
Don Zancanella
Western Electric